To all of the encouraging readers who write to me,
a great big "thank you!"

ELAINE L. SCHULTE is the well-known author of thirty novels for women and children. Over one million copies of her popular books have been sold. She received a Distinguished Alumna Award from Purdue University as well as numerous other awards for her work as an author. After living in various places, including several years in Europe, she and her husband make their home in Austin, Texas where she writes full time.

Cara and the
Terrible Teeners

T^{he} Twelve Candles Club

1. Becky's Brainstorm
2. Jess and the Fireplug caper
3. Cara's beach party Disaster
4. Tricia's Got T-R-O-U-B-L-E
5. Melanie and the Modeling Mess
6. Bridesmaid Blues for Becky
7. Double Trouble for Jess McColl!
8. Cara and the Terrible Teeners

Cara and the Terrible Teeners

Elaine L. Schulte

BETHANY HOUSE PUBLISHERS
MINNEAPOLIS, MINNESOTA 55438

Cover illustration by Andrea Jorgenson

Published in assocation with the literary agency of Alive
Communications, P.O. Box 49068, Colorado Springs, CO 80949.

Published by Bethany House Publishers
A Ministry of Bethany Fellowship, Inc.
11300 Hampshire Avenue South
Minneapolis, Minnesota 55438

Printed in the United States of America.

Library of Congress Cataloging-in-Publication Data

Schulte, Elaine L.
    Cara and the terrible Teeners / Elaine L. Schulte.
       p.   cm. — (The Twelve Candles Club ; 8)
    Summary: When someone tries to sabotage the Twelve Candles
Club, Cara suspects her half sister Paige and struggles to believe that
the truth will win out in the end.

    [1. Clubs—Fiction. 2. Moneymaking projects—Fiction.
3. Babysitters—Fiction. 4. Christian life—Fiction.] I. Title.
II. Series: Schulte, Elaine L. Twelve Candles Club ; 8.
PZ7.S3867Ca   1995
[Fic]—dc20   95–18995
ISBN 1–55661–536–1   CIP
                                                   AC

CHAPTER

1

Cara Hernandez clutched the letter as she rushed from her house. Not that she needed the letter, since its words were already imprinted in her head.

> The Santa Rosita Times *is pleased to inform you that you have won the $100 first prize in this year's "Young Writers' Contest." Your picture and fine article, "Twelve Candles Club Makes Fun and Money" will appear in Monday's Lifestyle Section of our newspaper. We hope it will bring your working club even more jobs this summer. We would especially like to applaud your skillful writing.*

The letter had arrived Thursday, but she'd been so stunned that she'd only told her family. Friday, a reporter and a photographer had come for an interview. Excited didn't describe how she felt. *Thrilled* was more like it. Best of all, her parents were too.

Only her half sister Paige Larson didn't like it. The words for Paige were *grouchy* and *jealous*, maybe even *looking for trouble, as usual*.

Cara hurried across the street.

"Hi, Cara!" yelled Tricia Bennett, the club's treasurer. She and Becky Hamilton, their president, rode their bikes toward her in the California sunshine. "We've got the newspaper!"

Cara's heart fluttered nervously. "All right! I brought the letter!"

This morning, she'd finally told them about winning the contest, and they'd been happy for her—not even jealous. But maybe her article wouldn't seem so good in print. And who knew what the reporter had written about her? People claimed you never knew what reporters might write, no matter what you told them.

She hurried up the driveway to Jess McColl's door for this afternoon's Twelve Candles Club meeting. Jess and Melanie Lin were baby-sitting in Israel with the church group. That left only three TCC members—Cara, Tricia, and Becky—to keep their club going here in Santa Rosita.

"Which key?" Cara muttered, and finally found Jess's on her key chain. Unlocking the door, she stepped into a three-car garage converted into a huge white room with a beamed ceiling and mini-blinds at the windows. Despite the twin beds and lots of expensive gymnastic equipment, the room seemed very empty with Jess gone off to Israel.

"Yipes!" Cara exclaimed. The answering machine light blinked endlessly, meaning lots of jobs for them. Well, they'd listen to the messages together and decide who'd get which job, unless clients asked for a certain club member.

She opened the mini-blinds at the front window, seeing Tricia and Becky hurrying along the sidewalk, their bike probably parked behind the garage as usual. Tricia's long reddish blond hair gleamed in the sunshine, and she swept along dramatically, as was perfectly natural for her.

By comparison, Becky was tall, thin, and a trifle klutzy. A blue headband matching her blue eyes held back her long brown hair. Both girls wore white shorts and matching blue and green Tees from Becky's birthday party.

It was at her birthday party where the idea for the Twelve Candles Club had started just two months ago. Even the club's name had come from the twelve candles on Becky's birthday cake.

Cara opened the door.

"Well, if it isn't the famous writer, Cara Hernandez!" Tricia called out, her green eyes sparkling. "It looks like a great article about you in the newspaper. Mom was at the supermarket when the papers were delivered and thought you'd want one before home delivery hit the streets."

"This is so exciting, Cara!" Becky added. "You made the front page of the Lifestyle section!"

"The front page!" Cara exclaimed, even more unnerved. "Have you read it?"

"Not yet," Tricia answered. "Mom just brought it home." She handed over the Lifestyle section of newspaper. "It's a great picture of you! And it'll probably bring the club even more business!"

Glancing at the paper, Cara felt peculiar to see her own heart-shaped face and brown eyes staring back from the top of the page. She was seated at her desk as if she were writing, and she wore the very same yellow Tee and white shorts she had on today. It seemed as if she were exposed for everyone in Santa Rosita to see.

"You look beautiful," Becky said as they glanced at the picture with her. "Just beautiful."

"Come on!" Cara objected. "If anything, I look shy."

"You don't either," Becky said. "You look like you're a thoughtful and interesting person."

"Maybe interesting," Cara decided.

"And beautiful," Tricia insisted.

Cara had to laugh. The truth was she didn't consider herself beautiful or cute or even pretty, but maybe sort of poetic and interesting looking like a writer should be.

To the right, a headline announced *Winning Article in the Young Writers' Contest.* On the other side of her picture it stated, *Cara Hernandez, Writer.* She started to read the interview article, her friends reading with her.

> *Twelve-year-old Cara Hernandez is not only a member of the enterprising Twelve Candles Club, but also a budding writer.*
>
> *Interviewed at her Santa Rosita home, Cara was unsure whether she would focus her writing on poetry, stories, or nonfiction, but one thing is certain: she is already a talented writer, as our readers will note from her winning article.*

"Aren't we always saying that God gave you a talent for writing?" Tricia asked.

Cara nodded. It was true, they often talked about God giving everyone at least one talent, but sometimes she'd felt unsure of it. Now here was the *newspaper* saying she had a talent for writing!

The article went on with minor details: she'd be going into seventh grade at Santa Rosita Middle School this fall . . . her parents owned Flicks Video . . . she'd lived in Santa Rosita for five years . . . and she was secretary of the Twelve Candles Club.

"I guess the article's all right," she decided. Thank goodness they hadn't mentioned that if she became a real writer, she might use her middle name and be Amelia Hernandez. It'd been dumb-dumb-dumb to tell them!

"The article's short and to the point," Tricia said.

"They were in a hurry," Cara explained. "Probably didn't have another story for the first page of the section today."

"Maybe they'd been saving that spot for whoever won the contest," Tricia said.

"Maybe," Cara answered. "I wonder if they changed my article." She read quickly,

TWELVE CANDLES CLUB
MAKES FUN AND MONEY

This summer there's been fun and extra money for the five twelve-year-old girls in the Twelve Candles Club.

The fun has come from helping at parties for kids and even for adults, not to mention housecleaning for interesting people, car-washing together, and a childcare program three mornings a week called "Morning Fun for Kids."

The Twelve Candles Club began in June at the start of summer vacation. It grew quickly because of free youth ads in the Santa Rosita Times *and an unexpected interview with the club president, Becky Hamilton, about a dog chase. The members also passed out artistic flyers about their work.*

For some of their most interesting jobs, they've worn cos-

tumes. They've dressed in polka-dotted clown costumes for kids' birthday parties, back-to-school clothes for a modeling job, and cowgirl outfits for a charity benefit for Casa de Ampara. *After the benefit, a picture and article about them appeared in the* Santa Rosita Times.

Usually, though, they wear ordinary clothes, especially for baby-sitting, car-washing, and housecleaning. As many as twenty younger children, ages four through seven, have come to their Morning Fun for Kids childcare program on Monday, Wednesday, and Friday mornings. Their guests are called Funners, and a special "Magic Carpet Ride" on a raggedy brown rug takes the Funners on imaginary visits to such places as the moon, the circus, a mountain campground, Catalina Island, and even a Chinese New Year's parade.

The club's five members are Becky Hamilton, President; Jess McColl, Vice-President; Tricia Bennett, Treasurer; Melanie Lin, Assistant-at-Large, and Cara Hernandez, Secretary. Jess and Melanie are currently baby-sitting children on the Santa Rosita Community Church's trip to Israel.

Whether it's in Santa Rosita or in faraway Israel, the Twelve Candles Club can't seem to help making money and having fun at it!

"They didn't change one word," Cara said.

"It's great!" Becky answered. "You've made us sound so good." She gave Cara a hug, then Tricia did, too.

Flustered, Cara felt heat rushing to her face. She babbled, "The contest rules said '225 words or less,' and it was hard to tell so much in so few words."

"Well, you did it," Tricia assured her. "Thank goodness

you didn't write that we're also known as Club El Wacko!"

They all laughed.

"Here's the letter they wrote me about winning," Cara said before they could gush too much more about her. It was wonderful, but she wasn't used to friends hugging her or being so proud of her.

The phone rang, and she was glad to have an excuse to dash for Jess's desk. On the other hand, maybe it was someone calling about the newspaper article already. "Twelve Candles Club," she answered.

No one spoke.

"Twelve Candles Club," she repeated.

No one answered this time, either.

"Is anyone there?" she asked uneasily.

Still no answer.

"What's up?" Becky asked, looking up from reading the newspaper's letter. "Don't tell me it's someone trying spooky phone calls on us again!"

Just then Tumbles "Burglar Catcher" McColl, Jess's brown chow puppy, barked in the backyard.

Putting the phone down, Cara breathed a soft "Yipes!" and raced for the back window. She peered out between two mini-blind slats in case a burglar was there. Jess's brown chow puppy was barking happily from his new doggy yard behind her room. No one was there. "I think Tumbles is just glad to have someone around."

She knocked at him on the window, and he barked wildly. "Look at him wag that tail! Probably he's been lonely with Jess and her parents gone and her brothers at work."

Cara let the mini-blinds flip shut and hurried back to the phone. Still nothing. "The phone call doesn't sound spooky, either . . . just no one talking." She passed the phone to Becky. "It's not a dial tone or busy signal . . . just quiet."

"Hello, this is the Twelve Candles Club," Becky said into the mouthpiece. "Hello . . . hello . . . hello?" She rolled her eyes. "Hello, this is the Twelve Candles Club. Who is this calling?"

After a moment, she put a hand over the phone. "Maybe it's a glitch in the phone lines."

Tricia took the phone and listened. "Let's just hang up," she decided, then did it. "Maybe it's kids being silly. Everyone knows we take calls each day from four-thirty to five-thirty. And now there's Cara's article in the paper."

Cara sat down on the edge of Jess's bed, her chest tightening. "Maybe the article attracted some crazies."

"Oh, come on!" Becky objected. "The article just came out, and almost no one has home deliveries yet." She grinned. "Besides, Tricia's supposed to be the dramatic one here!"

Cara felt a little better. "Well, let's listen to the answering machine messages. The light's sure blinking out lots of them."

She poked the "play" button, and the tape's robot-man voice stated, "You have twelve messages. Please wait."

"Twelve messages!" Cara said. "It must be filled up."

The tape rolled back forever, then finally clunked into place. The robot-voice announced, "Monday . . . one P.M.," followed by the same silence again. Another click sounded, and robot-voice proclaimed, "Monday . . . one-fifteen P.M." Another long silence was followed by a click.

Cara clenched her teeth as they listened to the other ten silent messages followed by clicks. "We need this phone to be working. If it's some kind of phone line trouble, it could ruin the club."

"I hadn't thought of that," Becky said. As president of the club, she settled unhappily in the oak desk chair. "It's the truth, though. We're tied to Jess's phone number for calls. Without her phone and answering machine, we're ruined."

"Exactly what I was thinking," Cara replied. "But I really do have a feeling it's because of my article . . . maybe from someone who has earlier home delivery." She almost told them that even Mom thought she was intuitive, meaning she often sensed what was going on before others realized it. *Sensitive,* Mom called it, too. Usually *too sensitive.*

"No way is it your fault," Becky objected. "Anyhow, the phone will be ringing madly any minute, so let's start the meeting first." She straightened her spine against the back of Jess's desk chair and announced in her presidential tone: "This meeting of the Twelve Candles Club shall now come to order. May we hear the minutes of the last meeting?"

Cara opened her secretary's notebook. "The last meeting of the Twelve Candles Club was on Friday, August 3, at Jess McColl's house. Old business. We discussed the weekend jobs and were reminded that Mrs. Terhune has switched her cleaning job to every other Saturday now that her baby is bigger. That means not this week, but next Saturday afternoon."

She read on. "New business. We noted that Jess and Melanie would be in Israel for nine days. Also that Becky will be living at her Gram's at the beach then, since her mom and new step-dad will be on the Israel trip. Her gram will drive her here for meetings and Morning Fun for Kids.

"Jobs such as Thursday cleaning for the Llewellyns and baby-sitting for the Davis twins and their cousins are off because they're in Israel. That should help cut our work load. Tricia reported $18.55 in the treasury. . . ."

She expected the phone to ring as it always did when she read the minutes of the meeting, but today there were no phone calls while she read all the way through "Respectfully submitted, Cara Hernandez."

In fact, they'd finished today's "treasurer's report," "old business," and "new business" before the phone rang again. This time Tricia picked it up. "Twelve Candles Club."

She listened, her green eyes growing more intent. Finally she said to Cara and Becky, "It's nothing again. I'll call the phone company." She clicked the phone and listened, then clicked four or five times. "It's still nothing. I can't even dial now."

"Didn't Jess say that her dad just switched phone companies to save money?" Cara asked.

"Come to think of it, she did," Becky answered. "Whoa! Maybe that's the trouble." She glanced at Cara. "Since you live closest, could you run home and try calling this number? At least we'd see if that works."

"Sure." Cara grabbed her key ring and ran, the back straps of her white sandals flopping. The Twelve Candles Club was the greatest thing in her life this summer—and now winning the Young Writers' Contest with her TCC article. . . ! They had to keep that phone ringing!

Outside, she noticed the newspaper man tossing copies of the *Santa Rosita Times* at driveways way up the street. It didn't take her long to cross their street, La Crescenta, to her family's small one-story white Spanish-style house.

She passed her half sister Paige's red Thunderbird on the driveway. Paige had spent every cent she'd inherited from her Grandmother Larson buying the car and flashy clothes—not to mention red carpeting and black lacquered furniture for her bedroom. Now she was probably out of gas money.

Cara unlocked the front door. "It's just me," she called into the house. She made her way to the kitchen archway. "I have to use the phone."

Paige put the phone to her black Tee to muffle her words. "I'm using the phone, as if you didn't notice!"

She wore one of her usual black and red shorts outfits, and a snobby look-at-me smile. For a change she had her long blond hair pulled back in a ponytail, too. Maybe because of the hot August weather or maybe because her naturally blond hair was nearly ruined from so much streaky highlighting.

"What happened to the personal phone line in your room?" Cara asked.

"I had it taken out a while ago," Paige answered, then ignored her as she listened to whatever someone on the other end was telling her. Probably one of her so-called friends who didn't know that cheerleader Paige Larson was out of money.

"I'll wait then," Cara said, "I have an important call. Actually, it's to the phone company. I'll bet they goofed up the neighborhood lines when they disconnected your phone."

Paige gave her a disgusted look, then said into the phone, "I'll call you later." She slammed it down. "Go ahead with your important call, *Caro-leen-a.*"

Cara ignored her, took the phone, and push-button dialed Jess's number. After a moment, the phone rang just fine, and Becky answered, "Hello, this is the Twelve Candles Club."

"Hey, it's working!" Cara exclaimed. "Maybe this phone call cleared the line. You know how weird phone lines can be at times. Besides, Paige just had her private line disconnected, and the worker might have messed Jess's up, too."

"Or cut through the line entirely," Becky suggested. "That actually happened when we moved into the neighborhood."

"Anyhow, we're set," Cara said. "Be back in a second."

Paige watched her hang up. "May I have the phone now that you're finished with your *important* call?"

"Sure," Cara answered. "Why not?" For a while this summer, Paige had showed signs of being friendly, but lately she'd returned to her old difficult self again.

"Adios, Caro-leen-a Hernandez," Paige called behind her.

"Cara or Caroline," Cara retorted, "although *Caro-leen-a* is actually the most beautiful. Besides, your Spanish pronunciation isn't good—and according to your report cards, your English isn't much better. Maybe if you were half Hispanic, you'd learn something about languages and other people, and wouldn't have to act so snooty."

Paige simply lifted her chin, turned her back, and picked up the phone again.

It was always tempting to say, *At least I have a father who didn't run off when I was a baby.* But that was too mean—and nobody *ever* discussed it.

Instead, Cara asked, "Aren't you supposed to start dinner since you're not working?"

"Don't worry, I've got a frozen lasagna in the oven and a poisoned lettuce salad cooling in the fridge."

"Sounds dee-licious," Cara answered as she headed for the front door. Things could be worse. At least Paige hadn't yelled her usual, *Whose slave do you think I am?*

Outside, she felt sorry about their arguments. At the church youth group, they'd been learning *a gentle word turns away wrath*. It meant talking nicely would keep others from getting mad. She'd have to try to do better at being a half sister herself.

When she arrived back in Jess's room, she said, "Thank goodness the phone is fixed!"

"But it isn't," Becky answered. "Since you called, it's been ringing and giving out no sound again."

"How could it work just a minute ago from my house, then stop again?" Cara asked.

"Maybe the other callers are farther away," Becky guessed. "No, that doesn't make sense."

"I don't like it," Cara said. "We promised Jess and Melanie that we'd keep the club going, no matter what."

Tricia raised her brows. "I'm *not* trying to be dramatic, but do you think someone's trying to sabotage the club?"

"Who'd want to?" Cara asked. "I can't think of anyone who'd want to ruin it."

Becky and Tricia shrugged unhappily, and Cara didn't like the trouble one bit.

CHAPTER

2

The moment Cara returned home, she hurried down the hallway to her bedroom. For one thing, she wanted to avoid Paige; for another, she was eager to reread her contest-winning article. Could it hold a clue to their phone trouble?

In the room, Angora, her white cat, looked up drowsily from the sunlit window seat.

"Hey, Angora, I won the newspaper contest! I actually won it! You'd think I could have a little while to enjoy it before trouble hit."

Angora blinked, closed her eyes, and went back to sleep.

Cara flopped onto her flowered bedspread and read the article again. There was nothing in it to cause trouble. The club's phone number wasn't even given.

The good news was that it still seemed like a good article—not that she deserved full credit. Mom had suggested listing everything the club did before starting the actual writing. And Dad had encouraged her over and over with, "Cara, you can do it! You can do it!"

She read the article again. Maybe she shouldn't have said "faraway Israel." "Faraway" sounded like a word from a little kids' picture book. Beyond that, the article was okay—and had earned her one hundred dollars!

She rolled over on her bed and thought that she might use some of the money to "help" her room. Paige called the decorating "stupido nothing," which meant tan carpeting, creamy walls, and creamy window shutters. There was also yard-sale maple furniture, a flowery quilted bedspread, and a matching window seat cushion upon which Angora had gone back to sleep.

Last week, she'd bought a natural wicker bird cage and filled it with peach, yellow, and coppery flowers to go with the bedspread. She'd hung the bird cage from the ceiling in the corner near her maple desk. It was a cheery touch, but the room was still unexciting. Maybe she'd use some of her winnings to buy bookshelves for over her desk.

She heard her father's Flick's Video van pull into the driveway and doors slamming. "Hey, here's the paper!" Dad exclaimed outside. "Cara's article should be in it!"

Cara guessed they'd be pleased with the article and her picture. Maybe God had really given her a talent for writing. But how could she know for sure, since she knew so little about Him? She remembered telling Paige early this summer, "I'm really going to become a Christian!"

Sure, she was going to the church youth group on Sunday mornings, but she hadn't really done anything else about it.

———

The smell of baked lasagna filled the dining area, and Cara's father beamed at her from beside her at the round table. "I'm so proud of you, Cara. I could almost burst without eating! Another scholar in the family, besides your mother."

His beautiful brown eyes were shining. His dark beard had grown out a little since this morning, but he still looked handsome. In fact, as far as she was concerned, Arturo Hernandez was the most handsome man in the neighborhood—and maybe even the nicest.

Mom looked proud, too. "Didn't I tell you to list everything the club does before writing the article? It's exactly how I try to write my class papers."

Mom wore a denim sundress instead of her usual jeans outfits. With her wavy dark blond hair and dreamy gray-blue eyes, she looked almost the same age as her classmates at the college where she was forever taking courses.

Across the table, Paige dug her fork into her lasagna. "If everyone's done congratulating Cara, let's eat."

Cara drew a breath, ready to ask, *Couldn't we try having a prayer?* But Dad was telling Paige, "You shouldn't be jealous. Instead, you should take pleasure in each other's honors. Cara's winning the contest brings honor to you . . . to this entire family."

Paige shot him a disgusted glance.

Cara chewed a piece of lettuce from her salad. She knew she didn't take much pleasure in Paige being a cheerleader, either. They always seemed at each other's throats. Maybe she should try to be nicer. It took an effort, but she made herself tell Paige, "You're a very good cheerleader."

Paige eyed her with suspicion.

"It's true—"

"A lot you know about cheerleading!" Paige retorted.

Cara felt a surge of anger. "Can't you even say thanks for a compliment? I don't think you've ever in your whole life told anyone 'thank you' unless you're reminded!"

"Girls!" Mom warned. "We've all had a busy day, and we've had our own challenges to deal with. Let's not do battle at the dinner table."

Everyone ate quietly for a while, and Cara felt as if her half sister had gotten the better of her, as usual.

Finally Dad asked Cara, "How's the club doing with Jess and Melanie gone?"

Cara lifted her shoulders, then dropped them. "We're having phone trouble. The answering machine was all filled up, but every message space was silent, then during the meeting whenever the phone rang there'd be nothing but silence."

"Did you call the phone company?" Dad asked.

"I guess I should have. I came home and called Jess's number and it worked." She glanced toward the living room, where the whirl-a-gig clock stood on the mantel. "It's six-thirty. The phone company will be closed. I'll have to call them first thing in the morning."

Dad frowned thoughtfully. "It sounds as if the phone must be all right if it's still ringing."

Cara forked up a chunk of lasagna from her plate. "I keep wondering if it's someone trying to mess up the club. I just have a bad feeling about it."

"Oh, come on!" Paige said. "You're always having feelings-feelings-feelings, and it's boring-boring-boring."

Cara ignored her.

Dad raised his brows. "I guess if someone actually wanted to mess up the club, they'd just have to call and leave their receiver off the hook."

Mom's blue-gray eyes filled with doubt. "Who'd want to do it, though?" She hesitated. "You don't suppose Jordan McColl is making those crazy phone calls again?"

"I don't think so," Cara answered. "These are different than the ones he did to be funny. Anyhow, I'll call the phone company in the morning. It probably has to do with Jess's father changing phone companies."

"You mean long-distance carriers?" Mom asked.

"Yeah, long-distance carriers."

Mom smiled. "A writer has to be careful about words."

Paige smirked across the table at her.

With Paige around, everyone has to be careful, Cara thought. If her half sister wasn't so lazy, not to mention busy with her so-called friends and boyfriends, she'd wonder if maybe Paige weren't making the phone calls herself.

In her bedroom, Cara tugged her journal from between her mattresses and opened it to the next blank page. Whoops . . . she hadn't written in it for a few days. Feeling guilty, she took a pen from her nightstand, then propped herself up against the bed pillows and wrote.

I still can't believe I won the Santa Rosita Times *Young Writers' Contest—and $100! For extra proof, though, the article is in today's newspaper, along with an article about me. Tricia and Becky are so happy for me, and I felt so good until I came home.*

Paige is the trouble, of course. Probably she's jealous and that's why she likes to ruin things. At least Mom and Dad are pleased. It's such a pain, though, for Paige to always stick pins into my bright happy balloon moments.

Other good news. I'll be able to buy the best back-to-school clothes I've ever had if we can keep the club going at top speed. Also, last month Dad made Paige return new clothes for refunds so she could give back the money she stole from my closet. I have most of that money left, too.

Not so good news. We're having phone troubles at Jess's house. Hmmmm . . . maybe I'll try calling her number when I finish writing here.

No job tonight. Even before the phone troubles, job requests were down because of vacations. Tomorrow morning, we work for Mrs. O'Lone down by the ocean. She's not fun like Mrs. Llewellyn, but we've been cleaning for her every Tuesday morning since the club began. It's a job we count on.

Think I'll try Jess's phone now.

Cara closed her journal, hid it between her mattresses again, and pulled the flowery bedspread down over it. Probably Paige wouldn't snoop there, since pulling up the mattress might break her precious fingernails.

In the living room, Mom and Dad were watching the TV news, and there was no sign of Paige anywhere. "I'm going to try to call Jess's phone now," Cara told them.

"Good idea," Dad answered.

In the kitchen, she turned on the light, then dialed Jess's phone number.

One ring, two rings, three rings, four . . . then Jess's voice. "This is Jess McColl and also the number for the Twelve Candles Club. Please leave your name, number, and message after the beep."

Cara waited, but instead of just one or two beeps, the answering machine beeped on and on. The tape must be filled up again. What was going on?

———

The next morning, Cara rode her bike up La Crescenta and arrived just as Tricia rode out the garage of her two-story peach-colored house.

"Hey, Cara!" Tricia sang out.

"Perfect timing!" Cara replied. "We're off!"

Tricia laughed. "Way off, as Jess would say."

Cara pedalled along on the street slowly, waiting until Tricia shut her garage door. Becky used to join them from her small Spanish-style house next door, but today she'd bike from her gram's condo to the O'Lone house. Already, an awful "For Sale" sign stood in Becky's front yard. As soon as her mom and new step-dad returned from Israel, Becky would be moving to the other side of town.

While Cara waited, Melanie Lin's aunt and uncle drove out of their cul-de-sac across the street. Auntie Ying-Ying opened her window and called out with her Chinese accent, "How's it doin', girls? How's it doin'?"

Cara grinned. "Fine, thank you!" With Auntie Ying-Ying, it was best to keep things simple.

"I think maybe-maybe I got big job for club!" Auntie Ying-Ying shouted. "Husband in hurry. Let you know soon!"

"Good!" Cara called back, then returned her excited wave. "See you!"

Just then, Tricia rode up on her bike. She waved to Auntie Ying-Ying, too, even though their car was already some distance away. "What kind of a job could we all do for her?"

Cara shrugged. "Probably nothing dull."

"You're right about that," Tricia said with a laugh.

They pedalled off together on their bikes. After a while Tricia asked, "Anything new about Jess's phone?"

"I called last night and Jess's voice came on, but then lots of beeps like the tape was filled up."

"Same here," Tricia said. "Well, maybe we can figure it out this afternoon when we're there."

"It's strange, though," Cara remarked.

"There's something else strange," Tricia said. "Mom said neighbors are receiving flyers about another working club in their mailboxes."

"You're kidding! Who are they?"

" 'Teeners' is what they call themselves."

"*Teeners*. . . ." Cara pronounced unhappily. "How old?"

"Sixteen to eighteen, and they make a big deal about their age, about being *mature* and having lots of experience."

"I can't believe it!"

Tricia nodded, her blondish red hair moving up and down over her green Tee's shoulders. "It looks to me as if others are trying to get our work."

"Do you think it's because of my article in the newspaper?" Cara asked, feeling even worse. "I'd hate to be the cause of trouble—"

"No way," Tricia answered, "I think it got started before that. Maybe two or three weeks ago, Mom thinks."

"Who's in it?"

"Leigh Warrick and Sandra Bassinger are the only names she heard."

"Uffffff!" Cara huffed. "More cheerleaders! As if I didn't have enough trouble with the one who lives in my house."

"You think Paige might be in it?" Tricia asked.

Cara shook her head. "She's too lazy to do hard work. . . . Now that I think of it, though, she does need money. But she's too lazy to take care of kids and clean houses. She'd run at the sight of a dirty diaper, and she's always saying, 'Whose slave do you think I am?' "

Tricia chuckled. "Can't say it surprises me," she said, then rode ahead in the bike lane on Ocean Avenue.

Cara was glad it was mostly downhill toward the ocean. Before long, they passed the *Santa Rosita Times* building, then the shopping center with Morelli's Pizza Parlor and Flicks.

Cara was glad to see six cars parked in front of her family's video store. That meant customers to rent videos or to use the FAX, photocopy machine, and other services. Dad had put in Flicks stores in Los Angeles, too, and even in Mexico, but it was taking a long time for them to get going.

Traffic along Ocean Avenue was heavy, as usual, and it was quite a while before they turned onto Mrs. O'Lone's street, overlooking the ocean. Before long they biked into the driveway of the white two-story Spanish house. It was a beautiful old house but had lots of nooks and crannies—and peeling paint around the windowpanes. No matter how hard you worked, it never looked perfect.

Tricia glanced back as they braked to a stop. "Here comes Beck around the corner!"

They parked their bikes and waited for Becky.

"Whew!" she said as she pulled up. "It's farther from Gram's condo than I thought."

They made their way to the front door and rang the bell.

Mrs. O'Lone was a thin older woman, and when she opened the door, she looked surprised to see them. "Didn't you girls get my letter?"

"What letter?" Cara asked.

"Why . . . the way mail delivery is, it may not be there yet," Mrs. O'Lone said. "But I've called and called your phone number, and there's no answering machine space or any one to answer." She drew a breath. "Well, the truth of it is that I've hired some older girls to clean for me on Tuesday mornings."

Cara swallowed hard. "Teeners?"

"Yes, I do believe that's what they call themselves," the woman said. "They've had handouts in the mailboxes and ads on the supermarket bulletin boards. They're very professional. I'm sorry you rode your bikes all the way out here for nothing. I'm truly sorry."

Tricia asked, "Didn't we clean your house well?"

"Why . . . yes, you did," Mrs. O'Lone admitted. "It's just that the Teeners are older . . . and they're not charging as much money." She glanced at her watch. "I'm afraid they're late, but they'll be here soon. Thank you again, girls." She nodded at them, then closed the door.

"Would you believe this?" Becky asked. "Would you believe this could be happening to us?!"

No one answered.

Finally Tricia said, "We may as well ride to the beach as long as we're this close. We don't have anything else to do now, and maybe just being by the ocean will make us feel better."

"May as well," Cara decided, and Becky agreed.

Before long they pedalled along in the bike lane on the Pacific Coast Highway, then onto the beach parking lot. They coasted to a stop at the bike racks and parked their bikes.

Catching her breath, Cara stood looking at the shimmering blue Pacific Ocean. The rumble of traffic on the highway had faded, replaced by the muffled sea roar. "I feel a little better already just seeing and hearing the ocean."

"Let's go walk along the beach," Becky suggested.

"And pray about this mess with the Teeners," Tricia added.

Down by the ocean, one wave after another rolled across the sand, soothing them even more. "Let's pray now," Becky said. "After all, the God who made this ocean and sky and sand can take care of a little problem like some competition. Tricia, you pray."

Cara bowed her head, not sure God would be concerned about small stuff like their jobs and the Teeners.

After Tricia asked God to help them know what to do about the Teeners, Becky echoed a loud, "Amen."

Cara added a doubtful, "Amen."

"I just thought of a great verse!" Tricia exclaimed, bouncing with excitement. " 'And we know that all things come together for good to those who love God and are called according to His purpose.' " She closed her eyes and breathed a "Thank you, Lord!" Looking up at Becky and Cara, she said, "You know, I think God is going to grow our faith through this trial!"

Their trouble "coming to good"? Cara marveled. It seemed not only crazy, but impossible.

Two hours later, the sun turned the sand hot, and they hadn't brought beach towels or blankets. They raced across the sant to their bikes and started for home.

"I'll ride along with you," Becky said. "Gram won't be expecting me back for a while."

"Let's go by Mrs. O'Lone's and get a look at these Teeners," Tricia suggested. "We can ride on the other side of the street and the trees will hide us a little."

"All right, I guess," Cara said.

They rode along, then turned onto the O'Lones' street. Suddenly Cara saw something horrible. "It's Paige's red Thunderbird! The Teeners must be Paige and her friends! They probably want to make money to have their hair bleached even more!"

As they neared the O'Lones' house, Cara saw Paige hanging out of an upstairs window, a bucket of water on the ledge. Below, Sandra Bassinger and Leigh Warrick washed a sliding glass door on the patio.

Cara was so angry, she yelled, "I thought you couldn't stand heights, Paige Larson! I should have known you'd pull something like this! Just wait till I tell Dad you've stolen our job. Stolen it from us!"

Paige looked right at her. "It won't be the last job we steal, either. We're older and more experienced!"

"You're not the least bit experienced about hard work!" Cara returned. "You're lazy beyond words!"

Paige flung an arm out angrily, bumping the bucket on the windowsill. She grabbed for the bucket wildly, sloshing water over herself, then down its other side onto Sandra and Leigh on the patio.

"Stop it!" they shrieked. "You've ruined our hair! Ruined it. . . !"

"Stop yelling at me!" Paige shrieked back. "I'm drenched too! If you weren't so scared of doing upstairs windows—"

Tricia and Becky started laughing, making their bikes wobble crazily. Cara had to stop her bike entirely. As mad as she felt, she clapped a hand to her lips to keep from laughing at her drenched half sister and her friends.

"Come on," she finally managed. "Let's get out of here!" All the way home, she replayed the water bucket spilling scene in her head to keep from being mad.

CHAPTER

3

Dear Journal,

I am still so mad at Paige that I could bite an alligator. If it weren't for the memory of the great water bucket bumble at the O'Lones' house, I'd probably go crazy. Let's hope there was lots of ammonia in the window-washing water like Mrs. O'Lone always wants. That'll ruin their precious hair!

When I think of all of the questions Paige asked in the last few weeks, it makes me even madder. Questions like "How much money do you get for Morning Fun for Kids?" She even asked, "Why don't you just show videos to keep the kids busy?"

I remember my exact answer about the videos. "Because we want it to be more creative and active. Morning Fun for Kids has to be special, so they'll beg their parents to come."

All the while Paige was asking questions, I thought she probably was nosing around so she could borrow money from me. Instead, she and her friends were plotting to ruin TCC. I even ex-

plained about crafts and snacks, and keeping money in the club treasury. I told Mom and Dad about everything the club has ever done—and now that I think of it, Paige was usually there taking it all in. So much for bragging!

One possible good thing: they can't do gymnastics like Jess does—or maybe they can since they're all cheerleaders! One good thing for sure: Sandra and Leigh seem to be about as lazy as Paige. Let's hope that doesn't change now.

Ohhhhhhhhhhhhhhhh, I am so mad. And I'll bet Tricia and Becky will say we have to forgive Paige and the others. How can I forgive Paige again and again when she makes me so mad? As for Tricia's "verse" about all things coming together for good, I don't see how this can ever be a good thing.

Bear, the youth minister at church, says, "Truth always wins out," but it's hard to imagine how the truth about the Teeners stealing our jobs will ever come out.

On top of everything else, TCC doesn't have a single job this afternoon, probably because of the phone trouble. I called the phone company, and they said whatever the problem might have been, it was fixed now. Let's hope so!

Anyhow, I'm so mad about the Teeners that I think I'll put all that mad energy to use and clean my room.

At four-thirty, Cara unlocked Jess's bedroom-gym door again. Jess probably wouldn't trust her again when she came home, Cara thought. Not with her own half sister trying to ruin the club. Inside, she glanced at the answering machine. The red light wasn't blinking at all!

What now?

Tumbles began to bark out back, probably glad for company after being alone all day long.

"Hey-hey, Cara!" Tricia and Becky sang out as they arrived in the room. In their white shorts and Tees they looked so great that Cara wished she'd worn hers instead of cut-offs and an old blue blouse.

They were surprisingly cheerful—probably to cheer her up, too. "You're taking this Teener stuff better than I am," she remarked.

"We'll just have to do better than the Teeners," Tricia said. "That's what Gramp says makes some businesses great—they do things *better* than others. You saw the water bucket disaster. It showed how *in*experienced the Teeners actually are."

"Maybe," Cara said. "Come to think of it, I'll bet Paige sloshed water into the house on the carpet, too. That wouldn't win them any points with Mrs. O'Lone."

Becky nodded. "We have to do our best and trust the Lord to work things out!"

Cara drew a breath. "Let's hope He's fixed the phone and the answering machine." She started past the gym equipment, heading for Jess's desk. "Look, there's not a single message on the answering machine now. Not a one!"

"Strange," Tricia answered. "I can't believe we wouldn't have at least one call."

Cara was the first to reach the machine, and she pushed the "play" button.

Nothing happened. Silence.

"I'll bet the tape is broken," Tricia guessed. "Dad had to change one of our tapes once, so I know it happens."

She flipped open the top of the tape holder. "See, it is broken! Maybe that's what was wrong with the phone yesterday. The broken tape affected the phone."

Cara didn't believe it. "Or maybe someone, like my dear half sister Paige, loaded the phone with so many calls that it broke down. Come to think of it, when I went home yesterday to call here, she was on the phone!"

Tricia took out the cut tape and inspected it. "I don't think getting too many phone calls can break a tape."

Cara didn't either. She glanced around the room. "You know, someone could have come in here and cut it!"

"Come on," Becky objected. "Tumbles would have barked. Besides, the neighbors all know Jess and her parents are in Israel, so Neighborhood Watch is on alert. And if anyone came at night, the boys are home."

"Maybe Jordan is trying to scare us again," Tricia said. "You know what he did that one time."

"Maybe," Cara replied. It was exactly what Mom had suggested. "The worst thing is Jess put me in charge of her room and gave me her key." She hesitated. "I'll have to come over tonight when they're home and ask Jess's brothers."

"Whoa! You sure you want to?" Tricia asked.

Cara shook her head. "No way do I want to, but I have to do it. Anyhow, even if they're not guilty, they should know if something's wrong. Maybe . . . maybe Dad would come with me."

"Good idea," Becky agreed. "Now let's try that phone."

Cara was closest, so she picked it up and listened. Silence. A spooky silence. "Nothing. No tone again! That means no new jobs for the club! We have to do something. . . ."

"We have to call the phone company again," Becky said.

She glanced at her watch. "Four forty-five! If you could do that, Cara, before the phone company office closes. Maybe this time you'd better call the repair section—"

"I'm off!" Cara answered and rushed for the door.

When she arrived at her house, no one was home. In the kitchen, she grabbed the phone book and flipped through the pages for the phone number. Finally on page 23! She dialed the number frantically.

"Repair Service Center," a man answered.

"I'm calling about a neighbor's phone that isn't working," Cara said. "There's no dial tone, nothing. . . ."

The voice sounded like robot-man on the answering machine. "What is the telephone number from which you're reporting the trouble?"

Cara gave her home number.

Next came, "Does the problem occur on all your phones?" Then, "Do you have a dial tone?"

Cara gritted her teeth. "No, that's what I told you."

"Is noise the problem on the line?"

Whoever it is must be reading a list of questions, Cara decided as she coped with "Can you call out? Can you receive calls? How often does the problem occur? Is the problem on local and/or long-distance calls?"

Finally the phone repair service said, "We'll check that line now." When he returned, he intoned, "We are receiving a busy signal. Please wait and try that number again." Having said that, he hung up.

Cara felt like screaming.

She punched in Jess's number herself. Busy! The only good thing she could think of was that at least Paige wasn't home, blocking TCC calls from this phone!

That night at dinner, Cara ate take-out oriental chicken with her parents. Paige was off baby-sitting.

"Who's she sitting for?" Cara asked, suspicious.

"A family named . . . ummmm, what was it?" Mom asked. "Carlton."

"Thank goodness!" Cara exclaimed. "I thought maybe it was another one of our clients. Paige and the other Teeners are trying to steal our jobs."

Dad lowered a forkful of rice. "What makes you think so?"

"This morning our Tuesday regular, Mrs. O'Lone, told us she'd hired other help. Then when we rode past her house later, we saw it was Paige, Leigh Warrick, and Sandra Bassinger!"

Mom remained quiet, but Dad asked, "Are you serious?"

Cara felt like crying. "I am! And Paige said it's not the last of our jobs they plan to steal, either."

"Paige actually said that?" he asked. "I can hardly believe she'd go that far—"

"She yelled it," Cara told him. "All of us heard. I think they mean to ruin our club . . . ruin it! And now Jess's answering machine tape is broken, and the phone isn't working, either."

"The answering machine problem can be solved easily, since we have some extra tapes," Dad assured her. "I'll go over with you and we can fix it right after dinner. I'll take a look at the phone, too."

"Good," Cara said, "because I have to ask Jess's brothers if they're causing the phone trouble. Jordan made the crazy phone calls that other time, and we thought—"

Mom raised her brows. "Cara, aren't you being over-sensitive about this entire job matter?"

"Oversensitive?" Cara echoed, looking at Mom's gray-blue eyes. "I . . . I can't believe you'd say that!"

"Now, Cara, be reasonable," Mom answered in her sensible tone. "Anyone can work wherever they find a job. We live in a free country."

"We live in a free country?!" Cara repeated, outraged.

She scarcely knew she was rising from the table. Suddenly she stood waiting for her mother to somehow smooth matters over . . . to say she didn't mean it.

But Mom only shook her head as if Cara were being childish.

"Excuse me!" Cara cried as she raced from the room. "Please excuse me from the table!"

———

Here I am again, journal. I am so mad and hurt and upset that I have to get it out of me. The problem now is that Mom is siding with Paige, saying anyone can work wherever they find a job, that we live in a free country!

Why does she always side with Paige instead of being fair? Maybe it's because she divorced Paige's father and feels guilty about that. Sometimes she slips and calls Paige's father "Mad Dog Larson," so I know she and Paige had a bad time. He drank a lot and was very mean to them. I'm sorry for them, but I wish they wouldn't take it out on me! It's not fair! It's not my fault he was rotten!

If it weren't for my friends in the Twelve Candles Club, I don't know what I'd do—

"Cara, you ready to go with me to Jess's?" her father asked outside her bedroom door. "I've got a replacement tape."

"Just a minute!"

"I'll wait for you out front," Dad said.

"I'll be right there!"

Have to go now, Cara wrote, then lifted her bedspread and stuck the journal back between the mattresses.

Outside, she found her father pulling a few weeds near the front door as he waited for her.

"Ready?" she asked.

To be funny, he straightened his back like a stiff-backed old man. "Ready if I can make it across the street."

Cara had to smile a little.

"Seriously, *amiga,* I'm concerned about the phone trouble. Maybe we can figure out what's wrong."

At least his caring made her feel better. And she liked it when he called her *amiga,* his voice warm and cozy.

They started across the street toward Jess's house, the biggest and nicest house in the neighborhood. As they looked up to the top of the driveway, Jess's seventeen-year-old brother, Jordan, was heading for the garage, his curly red hair bright in the sunshine.

It was no time to be shy, Cara told herself. "Hey, Jordan! Can we talk to you?"

"Hi, Cara," he answered, grinning and friendly as ever. "Hi, Mr. Hernandez. What's doing?"

When they arrived up by the garage, Cara was slightly out of breath. She glanced at her father.

40

"You explain it," he told her. "You're the club member and in charge of Jess's room."

Cara drew a breath and looked at Jordan. "We . . . that is, Jess's phone has been acting peculiar . . . you know, when we come for the TCC meetings. It rings and when we answer, there's no one on, only silence. And the answering machine is acting strange, too. In fact, the tape's broken now, so Dad is going to put a new one in for us. Anyhow, we . . . uh . . . wondered if you or your brothers knew . . ."

Jordan rolled his blue eyes skyward. "You're wondering if we're making spooky phone calls like I did before?"

Cara gave an embarrassed nod.

His face turned red. "No way! I'll ask Mark and Garn, but I don't think they'd do it. They already told me they think I was j-u-v-e-n-i-l-e."

Cara felt embarrassed herself. "Well, thanks. We'll just put the new answering machine tape in now if that's okay."

"Sure." He gave a nod at her dad. "Thanks for taking care of it, Mr. Hernandez."

"My pleasure," Dad said. "It's kind of your family to let the girls use Jess's phone."

Jordan cast a glance toward Jess's door. "Anything else wrong in there, like when we had the burglar?"

Cara shook her head. "No, nothing. Anyhow, Tumbles is back there now, and he yips when we come for meetings. I think he's glad when we're here."

"Yeh, I just fed him a while ago. Everything was fine back there." Jordan looked as if he'd run out of things to say, and just then, his brothers, Garner and Mark, came out the front door.

"Hey, you guys," Jordan called over to them. "Have you

41

been messing with Jess's phone or answering machine?"

Garner was eighteen, and handsome as could be with his reddish brown hair and broad shoulders. As if that weren't enough, he'd been captain of the Santa Rosita High football team last year. "*Come on!* I've got better things to do."

Sixteen-year-old Mark had awful red hair, lots of freckles, and was skinny as a stick. "No way! We don't even go near Jess's room. Dad's orders."

Jordan raised his pale red brows. "I think they're innocent," he told Cara and her father. "Well, hope you can figure it out. See you."

"Yeh, see you," Cara answered, then exchanged "See you's" with Mark and Garner.

They *saw her* as a little nuisance, she decided, which was all right in a way. But she understood why the high school girls chased after Garner. She'd overheard Paige and Sandra Bassinger wishing he weren't so interested in going off to college—and in smart girls who were going to college, too.

"Come on, *amiga*," Dad said, and they started for Jess's door, Cara digging for the key in her shorts pocket.

Inside, everything in Jess's bedroom-gym looked fine.

"Well, isn't this an interesting room!" Dad exclaimed, never having seen it before. "It's sure full of gymnastic equipment!"

"It sure is."

He looked at Cara for an instant as if wondering whether she were jealous.

"Don't worry, Dad, I don't want gymnastic equipment."

"Thank goodness for that. It must cost a fortune."

"I guess so. The phone's over here, by Jess's desk."

It took only a minute for him to replace the answering machine tape.

"Let's hope that fixes matters." He picked up the phone and listened. "There's a regular dial tone now." He handed the phone to Cara.

She listened. "Sounds fine. Maybe the answering machine was goofing up everything somehow."

"I suppose anything's possible," he answered, "but I don't see how."

"Me neither," she replied. "I don't see how."

————

When she returned home, Mom called out from her bedroom, "Cara, phone call for you!"

"Thanks!" Cara hurried to the kitchen phone. "Hello?"

"Cara, it's me, Tricia. Have you read today's *Santa Rosita Times*?"

"No. Afraid I usually don't."

"Me neither. Mom saw it. Go get it, the editorial section, page fourteen," Tricia said. "There's something about us in letters-to-the-editor, and it's not good."

Cara's heart sank. "Hold on."

She ran to the living room and grabbed the newspaper from the coffee table. Thumbing through the pages, she found page fourteen, then the letters-to-the-editor.

Returning to the kitchen, she picked up the phone. "I've got the page."

"Read the letter called 'Workers Too Young?' "

Cara saw it and began to read nervously

WORKERS TOO YOUNG?

Your article in Monday's paper about the twelve-year-old girls and their Twelve Candles Club encourages girls who are too young to care for children or do the other work mentioned. It is wrong of you to recommend these young girls by awarding one a $100 prize and encouraging them in any way. There are older, more mature workers available who need jobs.

T. L. Thompson

"I can't believe it!" Cara exclaimed.

"Who's T. L. Thompson?" Tricia asked. "Do you suppose it's really an older person who can't get a job?"

"I don't know. . . ."

"I think the Teeners are behind this," Tricia said. "I guess we'll have to call the paper tomorrow and ask them about T. L. Thompson. It's probably too late today."

"I guess so. But it doesn't sound like Paige's writing. Not with words like *encouraging, recommend,* and *available.* Her vocabulary doesn't go that far."

Tricia sighed. "I've got a feeling that maybe the three of them—Paige, Leigh, and Sandra—could have written the letter together if they really tried."

"Maybe," Cara decided, though Leigh and Sandra didn't seem smart either. "Anyhow, we'll call the paper tomorrow, but that letter sure won't be helping the Twelve Candles right now!"

"It's bound to be bad for the club," Tricia agreed.

"I feel sick about it," Cara said, "especially since Paige heard what we were doing right in my house. I should have been suspicious when she took such an interest in us."

"It's not your fault," Tricia assured her. "Let's think

about what we should say when we call the newspaper tomorrow morning. Maybe we ought to write something down so we don't say the wrong thing and get in worse trouble."

"Good idea," Cara said. "I feel terrible about that, too . . . especially since they've given me a hundred dollars."

"No amount of money gives them any right to print a letter that lies about us!" Tricia answered.

"You're right about that," Cara replied. "Maybe that's what we should tell them when we call, but in a nicer way."

Tricia gave a laugh through the phone. "You mean not call T. L. Thompson an outright liar?"

Cara had to smile herself. "Probably not."

"We'll have to phone them early . . . before Morning Fun for Kids," Tricia said. "Maybe eight o'clock. Let's each jot something down right now, then discuss it."

Cara reached for the note paper and pen on the kitchen counter and decided it'd be best to start with something positive. She cradled the phone between her ear and shoulder and began to write.

The Twelve Candles Club wants to thank you for using the article I wrote about them, and for awarding me the $100 prize for the Young Writers' Contest. We're suspicious, though, about the letter-to-the-editor from T. L. Thompson. We think maybe it's from another working club that wants us to look bad. Can you please check this T. L. Thompson? Is it a real person or could someone have made the name up?

"What have you written?" Tricia asked on the phone, and Cara read it to her.

"Sounds a lot better than mine," Tricia said. "Anyhow, I think you're probably the one who has to call them, since you won the prize and they did the article about you—"

"I know it," Cara answered unhappily. "I'll call them around eight-thirty tomorrow morning."

"I'll pray for you," Tricia said. "Becky and I will."

"I'll need it. Anyhow, see you at Morning Fun for Kids. Let's hope some kids show up."

"They will," Tricia promised. "Our regulars will be there, no matter what."

I hope so, Cara thought. "See you," she said again, then hung up the phone.

As if their telephone problems and the Teeners hadn't been bad enough! Now everyone in town would doubt whether Twelve Candles Club girls were old enough—and experienced enough—to take care of children.

Probably people would wonder if they could do other jobs, too! And on top of that, she'd have to call the newspaper and question them about the letter-to-the-editor. It just wasn't fair!

CHAPTER

4

The next morning, Cara waited until she was alone in the kitchen, then hurried to the phone. She dialed the *Santa Rosita Times* and asked for the letters-to-the-editor person. She'd already practiced what to say, and she had her notes in front of her.

On the other end of the phone a man said, "Editorial."

"This is . . . Cara Hernandez," she answered. She rushed on nervously. "Monday there was an article about me winning the Young Writers' Contest."

"Oh, you want Lifestyle—"

"No, I need to talk to you," Cara said quickly. "It . . . it concerns a letter-to-the-editor about the Twelve Candles Club in yesterday's paper. The title of the letter is *Workers Too Young?*"

"Then you have the right person. How can I help you?"

"Well, we're suspicious about the person who wrote the

letter. We think maybe it's from another working club that wants us to look bad so they can get our jobs. Can you check this T. L. Thompson?"

"Sure," the man said. "Please hold."

It was a moment before he returned to the phone. "We always phone the letter-to-the-editor writers, but somehow we missed this one. If you'll wait a little longer, I'd like to look at something else."

"Okay." Cara waited.

Finally the man returned to the phone. "We don't know how it happened, but we have no information on this letter writer. I can't imagine how it happened."

Cara wondered if the Teeners knew someone at the newspaper who could have stuck in the letter. She had no proof—

"You have our apology," the man was saying. "We'll print a retraction in today's paper. Will that be helpful?"

"Yes, I guess so," Cara decided. She clenched her fists with anger. "Thanks for checking."

The man apologized again, but Cara had a feeling that the damage to TCC would be hard to undo.

———

She still felt a little angry as she rode her bike to Tricia's house for Morning Fun for Kids. It was almost nine o'clock, and the usual sign was taped up on the gate.

MORNING FUN FOR KIDS
PLEASE KNOCK ON GATE

Cara parked her bike in the garage and headed out the side garage door into the breezeway. The sign-in card table

48

was already set up, with clipboards and name tags on it.

So far, Morning Fun for Kids, also known as "MFK," had been great fun. On Monday, Wednesday, and Friday mornings from nine to noon, they had play-care for kids aged four to seven. The kids were called Funners instead of kids, though.

Despite everything, Cara thought the Bennetts' fenced yard was perfect for MFK. The neat and spacious yard held a colorful gym set, swings, a sandbox, and a tree house in the overgrown California pepper tree.

The redwood picnic table and benches on the patio were great for Becky's arts and crafts, and the fresh peach color of the two-story house made everything seem colorful and welcoming. A lively tune about a "turkey in the hay and turkey in the straw" bounced from the patio speakers.

For their farm theme, Cara had worn jean cut-offs and tied a red bandanna handkerchief around the neck of her white Tee. As planned, Tricia and Becky wore matching outfits. The Funners had been told to dress for Farm Day, too. And, to add to the mood, a borrowed full-sized, black-and-white spotted cow painted on wood stood propped against the house.

"Cara!" Becky called out from the picnic table. "How did the newspaper phone call go?"

"They hadn't checked out the letter writer, which they usually do. So they're going to print an apology in this afternoon's paper."

"Thank goodness," Tricia said.

Cara shook her head. "I'm not sure it'll help."

"Well, it's better than nothing," Tricia answered. "What did they have to say about it?"

Cara shook her head. "They didn't know how the letter slipped past, but I'll bet the Teeners somehow got it by them."

"That wouldn't surprise me," Becky said.

"Not me, either," Tricia added.

Cara managed to get out, "I . . . I thought you might blame me."

"No way!" Tricia said.

Becky added, "It wasn't your fault! Gram says newspapers are always in a hurry to get out the day's paper. That's one reason they make mistakes. And we shouldn't believe everything we read in them, either."

Relieved, Cara felt a little less upset.

"Look at the little balsa wood cows Gramp cut out for crafts," Tricia said. "He even spray-painted them white. The Funners just have to paint the eyes, nose, and black spots."

It was a relief to have the subject changed, and Cara saw the thin wooden cow shapes lying on the table. "The Funners' parents will be impressed!"

"We hope so," Tricia said. "We'd better get to work." She handed Cara the day's schedule, which read,
AFTER PARENTS SIGN FUNNERS IN

1. Magic Carpet Ride (Tricia. Eee-iii-eee-iii-ooo! Becky and Cara to tie red bandannas around Funners' necks to add to the fun.)
2. Cow cutouts to paint for crafts (Becky)
3. Wagon rides (Tricia and Cara)
4. Midmorning snacks (Cara)
5. Farm video (Tricia in charge)
6. Free time for swings (All in charge)

"How come we're having a video?" Cara asked. She'd just told Paige that they never showed videos!

"Because Jess isn't here to do gymnastics," Tricia explained. "With her and Melanie gone, we had to fill in with something. It's not as if we always have videos. It's our first one. Besides, some of the Funners may never in their lives have seen a farm, not here in southern California."

"It's probably a good idea for today," Cara decided. "Where did you get a farm video?"

Tricia laughed. "Gramp got it at Flicks. Where else would we rent a video?"

Cara had to smile herself. "I didn't know we had any."

A moment later, cars stopped out front and doors began slamming. "Here come the Funners!" Cara warned. "Here they come!"

As usual, Becky went to greet the first kids since she was president. Tricia went next, because that's how they'd done it since the beginning. Cara was glad to be last so she could settle down more from the newspaper phone call.

Inside the house, Mrs. Bennett had changed the tape to "Old MacDonald Had A Farm," and *eee-iii-eee-iii-ooo's* floated from the patio speakers, filling the backyard.

Tricia's five-year-old brother, Bryan, tore out the kitchen door, followed by Amanda, Becky's five-year-old sister, and Suzanne, Tricia's seven-year-old sister. The Bennett kids attended MFK free because Tricia's mother helped and hung around in case of emergencies. Amanda came free, too, because she was Becky's sister and, at first, her family couldn't afford to pay.

Cara hurried to the breezeway, glad that the *eee-iii-eee-iii-ooo's* still floated across the yard from the patio speakers.

The next Funner to arrive would be hers to check in. She grabbed the clipboard from the card table just as someone knocked at the gate.

"Coming!"

Opening the gate, she saw seven-year-old Craig Leonard and his mother. "Hi!" Cara said to both of them.

She turned to Craig. "Welcome again to Morning Fun for Kids!"

But Craig was too busy glancing around the yard to answer. "Thank you," Mrs. Leonard said. "Craig's looking forward to Farm Day. He wanted to wear his jeans, and we found him that old straw hat. He always enjoys dressing up for your special days."

"He looks exactly right, too," Cara remarked.

Finally Craig smiled.

"We have red bandanna neckerchiefs for everyone," Cara added. "They're left over from one of our other days. And we have balsa wood cows to paint for crafts—"

"Is Jess back?" Craig interrupted.

"Not yet."

Craig's face fell. "I like gymnastics best."

"She'll be back from Israel next Monday," Cara told him. "Meanwhile, we'll have lots of other kinds of fun. It'll be a fun morning."

Craig looked unsure of it.

Mrs. Leonard quickly filled in the form, giving FUNNER'S NAME, AGE, and TIME IN. She left TIME OUT blank, and the rest—PARENTS' PHONE, DOCTOR'S NAME/PHONE NUMBER—she'd filled in the first time she'd brought Craig.

In the meantime, Cara printed "Craig Leonard" on two

name tags. "Look," she told him, "we have straw hat stickers on the name tags, almost like your straw hat. I'll bet Mrs. Bennett bought them. She always makes everything more fun."

He brightened slightly, and Cara stuck a name tag on the front of his T-shirt and another on the back. Next, she tied a red bandanna around his neck. "Hey! Look at the cow in the backyard!"

Craig glanced around. "It's not a real cow."

"No," Cara agreed, "but we can pretend, can't we? Pretending can be fun."

Mrs. Leonard remarked to Cara, "That was such a nice article you wrote to win the newspaper contest . . . and a nice article about you, too. But what on earth was that letter-to-the-editor all about?"

"We . . . ah . . . think another working club wrote it so they could steal our business," Cara explained. "The newspaper is printing an apology this afternoon."

"I should think they would!" Mrs. Leonard said. "Well, isn't that nervy?!"

"That's what we thought," Cara answered.

"I wonder if it's the same group who left a handout in our mailbox."

"Someone left a handout in your mailbox?!" Cara exclaimed.

Mrs. Leonard nodded. "The Teeners, I think they called themselves."

"You're kidding! That's . . . that's who we think wrote the letter, too," Cara answered.

"Their prices are lower than yours for their morning daycare."

"They're having a morning daycare, too?" Cara asked, her heart sinking.

"They are," Mrs. Leonard answered.

"I can't believe it. I can't believe they'd do it!"

"It seems that they are," Craig's mother answered. She turned to her son. "Well, you have a good time, even if Jess isn't here."

He nodded, and she headed for the gate.

"Where are all the Funners?" he asked Cara.

The yard did look a lot emptier than usual—only three Funners besides Amanda, Bryan, and Suzanne. Most of them wore jeans, and all of them now wore their red bandannas. "I expect they're still coming," Cara told him.

But no more car doors were slamming out front. "Come on," she said to Craig. "We're going to have lots of fun. Let's get out the Magic Carpet."

They went to the garage and, moments later, carried out the roll of brown raggedy carpet. "Where are we going on the Magic Carpet?" Craig asked.

"I'd guess it has something to do with a farm," Cara said. "What do you think?"

"I'd rather go to the moon or to the circus," Craig answered.

"Well, we'll see, won't we?" she asked.

He didn't reply. And he still didn't look very excited as they rolled out the long, narrow rug.

"Hey, everyone!" Tricia called out, "I want you all to meet a first-time Funner, Pinky Royster. Pinky is five years old and he's staying next door with the Cooblers. Let's give our new Funner a real welcome!" She clapped her hands and yelled, "Yeahhhhh, Pinky . . . yeahhhh, Pinky!!!!!"

Cara turned, clapping and yelling a "Yeah!" herself. It wasn't something they usually did, but it felt good to do . . . especially for someone named Pinky Royster. She glanced over the other kids to see who he might be.

He turned out to be a pink-faced boy with thin blond hair sticking up wildly. He wore denim bib overalls, so he must have known today was Farm Day. He wore a red bandanna, too. Probably Tricia had tied it around his neck. He didn't wear a shirt under the baggy bib overalls, and he was barefooted.

Pinky grinned at the applause, all the while sneaking a hungry glance at the snacks on the table. Suddenly he turned a somersault on the Magic Carpet, his bare feet flopping over.

"Yeahhhh, Pinky!!!!" Tricia called out again.

Pinky turned another somersault.

"Yeahhhh, Pinky!!!!" everyone yelled.

Pinky grinned from upside-down on the rug and turned another somersault, then another and another.

He sure is a somersaulter, Cara thought. And there he went again and again!

"With Pinky here, who needs Jess?!" Tricia laughed.

The nosy Coobler boys next door hung their heads over the fence. "What's that crazy kid up to?" nine-year-old Cody yelled as loud as he could.

Ten-year-old Doug shouted, "Look at that! It's the somersault kid!"

"Never mind, you two!" Tricia called back at them. "If you want to be part of Morning Fun for Kids, you'll have to pay for it like everyone else."

"No way!" the Coobler boys yelled back. "We're going to watch free of charge."

Cara gave them a don't-be-so-nosy look and shouted, "It's only for kids four to seven!"

"That's us!" Cody Coobler answered in a silly voice. "We're only four years old!"

"You're not," Becky told them. "You're nine and ten. Can't you find anything better to do?"

"Can't think of anything better than watching the somersault kid!" Cody answered.

Luckily, "The Farmer in the Dell" wafted across the yard from the patio speakers, and a few kids sang out, "Hi-hoh-the-dairy-oh, the farmer in the dell!"

None of it seemed to affect Pinky Royster. He changed direction, somersaulting back down on the Magic Carpet, his bare feet flying, his face even pinker.

"Come on," Tricia told everyone. "It's time for our Magic Carpet ride."

The Coobler boys mimicked in silly voices, *Time for our Magic Carpet Ride, kiddos. Time for our Magic Carpet Ride.*

Cara ignored them.

In charge of the back of the rug, she told Pinky, "Maybe you can somersault more later. We're going to go on a wonderful ride on the rug now. Okay? You can sit right here."

To Cara's relief, Pinky stopped somersaulting. His pale blue eyes took in the other six Funners settling on the raggedy brown rug, and he sat down behind them.

The Coobler boys called out again, *Time for our Magic Carpet Ride, kiddos. Time for our Magic Carpet Ride.*

Cara asked Pinky, "Why are you staying at the Cooblers' house?"

Pinky just rolled his eyes, then wobbled his head.

She decided he might be the Coobler boys' cousin, but they were both dark-haired. He sure didn't look like them. At least Mr. and Mrs. Coobler were very nice, so Pinky only had to put up with the two boys. She'd no more than thought it when Mrs. Coobler yelled at her two boys. "You boys get in here!"

"Oh, Mom!!!!!!!!!!!" they wailed.

"Don't you 'Oh, Mom me!' " she told them. "Don't bother those children, or you're going to have to answer to your father for it. Do you hear?"

Without even looking, Cara could tell by the sound of their voices that the boys were going inside. Thank goodness for that!

At the front of the Magic Carpet, Tricia raised her arms. "Before we go sailing away on the Magic Carpet, we should know each other's names," she told them. "Now, I know we all have name tags, but not all of us can read yet. Let's call out our names and tell how old we are."

"Craig Leonard!" Craig called out. "Seven years old!"

"Bryan Bennett! Five years old!"

Amanda Hamilton and Suzanne Bennett and the others yelled their names and ages, but Pinky Royster didn't say a word. Finally Tricia called out, "And at the back of our Magic Carpet is our new Funner, Pinky Royster, who's five years old. Welcome, everyone!"

Cara noticed that Pinky smiled a little. She just hoped he wouldn't start somersaulting up the rug while the other Funners were on it. Unfortunately it also struck her that it hadn't taken long for only six kids to tell their names and ages. It was nothing like the time it took when there were twenty Funners.

As usual, Tricia flung out an arm and closed her eyes. "Okay, Funners, close your eyes, too, and get ready for takeoff! Harrrummmm . . . harrummm. . . . T-a-k-e o-f-f! T-a-k-e o-f-f! Here we go in the a-i-r. Hold on to the Magic Carpet! H-o-l-d o-n!!!"

Cara had to smile, but she closed her eyes in case any of the Funners glanced at her. One thing about Tricia—even on a raggedy old carpet, she had a commanding presence. She made it seem as if they were really taking off into the air. Maybe it was because she acted in church skits and community plays.

"Harrrummmm . . . harrummmm . . . !" Tricia roared. "We're flying through the air . . . flying over my house, flying over the neighborhood . . . now flying over all of Santa Rosita. . . . What's that body of water we see?"

"The Pacific Ocean!" called out her sister, Suzanne.

"R-i-g-h-t-o!" Tricia answered. "Where do you Funners think we're going?"

"To a farm?" Craig Leonard guessed.

"R-i-g-h-t-o . . . to a f-a-r-m!" Tricia answered. "Very good guessing. Let me know when the first one of you sees a big red b-a-r-n."

"I see it . . . I see it!" yelled Amanda Hamilton, who was used to Magic Carpet rides.

"S-u-r-e e-n-o-u-g-h!" Tricia answered. "Let's slow down this zooming M-a-g-i-c c-a-r-p-e-t so we can fly over slowly. "Who sees some farm animals?"

Bryan Bennett yelled, "I see a cow! A black-and-white cow!"

"R-i-g-h-t-o!" Tricia answered. "What else do you see?"

Someone yelled, "Horses!"

"Chickens. . . !"

"Turkeys!"

"Pigs!"

"Sheep!"

"Goats! Lots of goats!"

Someone shouted, "There's no goats on farms!"

"Sure there are!" Tricia answered. "That's how we get goat milk and goat cheese! Listen! What are they saying?"

"M-o-o-o-o!" Bryan answered.

"That's cows!" his older sister said. "Cows say 'moooo,' not goats!"

Tricia called out, "What do those goats down there say?"

"Baaaaaa!" someone guessed.

"That's sheep!" Suzanne argued.

"Does a-n-y-o-n-e know what goats say?" Tricia asked.

No one answered and Cara didn't know either. She neighed "Wheee-eee-eee!" like a horse to be funny, and everyone laughed, just as she'd hoped.

She had to smile. Actually Morning Fun for Kids was fun for her, too. At first she'd dreaded it, probably because she had no younger kids in her family and she hadn't known how much fun—and trouble—they could be. Of course, it was easier this morning with so few Funners.

"Look at that tractor in the field," Tricia was saying. "Look at the dust flying! What's growing in that field?"

"Tomatoes?" Craig guessed.

"Yes, a whole field of t-o-m-a-t-o-e-s!" Tricia answered. "Acres and acres of tomatoes! And acres and acres of corn!

Now what's that growing in the vegetable garden?"

"More tomatoes and corn!" Becky yelled to be funny, too.

"Carrots and peas and beans!" Suzanne answered.

Pinky Royster still hadn't said a word. Cara was tempted to open her eyes, but one of the Funners might turn around and see her. Magic Carpet was like acting. You couldn't spoil the pretending for anyone, even if they peeked.

Finally they were leaving the farm on the Magic Carpet and landing back in Santa Rosita. Maybe going to a farm hadn't been as exciting as some of their other Magic Carpet rides, Cara thought but it was different for most of them.

"T-o-u-c-h d-o-w-n!" Tricia called out. "T-o-u-c-h d-o-w-n in the Bennett yard!" After a moment, she said, "Well, here we are! You can open your eyes now, Funners!"

Cara opened her eyes, then could hardly believe what had happened right in front of her.

Pinky Royster was gone!

She looked around the yard, but there was no sign of him. Suddenly she realized that raisin packs were missing from the redwood table—but that was nothing compared to their losing him. If anything else terrible happened to the Twelve Candles Club—they would be ruined for sure!

CHAPTER

5

"What happened to Pinky?" Cara asked.

Everyone looked to the back of the Magic Carpet rug, as surprised as she was to find him gone.

Tricia called out, "Let's look all over the yard. Everyone search! He couldn't reach the gate latch, so there's no way he could get out of the yard that way." She started toward the house. "I'll go alert Mom."

They spread out, and Craig even climbed up into the pepper tree to look around, but no one saw Pinky. It was a frightening moment, and for an instant, Cara thought maybe her imagination had gotten the better of her. Maybe she'd imagined him somersaulting on the rug. But could all of them have imagined Pinky being there?

Tricia rushed out. "He's not in the house, either!"

Just as everyone panicked, Mrs. Bennett opened the kitchen window. "Pinky's fine," she informed them. "Don't worry. It's all under control. Go on with Morning Fun for Kids."

"But how did he get out?" Tricia asked.

"I'll tell you later," her mom answered, then closed the kitchen window.

"It must be a secret," Craig Leonard remarked.

It sure must be, Cara thought in agreement.

The Funners asked a lot of questions, but Tricia finally got them quieted down. "Come on, Funners. It's time to draw cows. Wasn't it nice of my gramp to cut these cows out and paint them white? Becky's going to show you how to draw eyes on them . . . and big black spots."

After a while, the Funners settled down and painted black spots on the balsa wood cows. When they finished, there were "farm wagon rides" in Bryan's wagon, then mid-morning snacks of apple juice, raisins, and peanut butter crackers. Through it all, though, Cara couldn't stop worrying about Pinky Royster.

Before long, they trooped inside and settled on the family room floor to watch the cartoon video about farms, farm animals, and growing crops. It was funny—and more interesting than Cara thought it could be.

When the video ended, the Funners ran outside to the swings for free play. Finally, car doors slammed out front and parents were coming to get their Funners, who proudly carried their black-and-white "cows."

Leading the Funners to the gate, Tricia announced, "Friday will be Pet Day. Remember how you've all been asking to bring your pets? Well, Friday will be Pet Day! Be sure to tell your friends to bring their pets!"

Pet day? Cara's mind echoed, before she decided it was a great idea.

"Pet Day! Pet Day!" Bryan yelled excitedly.

"What if we don't want to?" Craig asked.

"No one has to," Tricia replied. "Only if you want to, you can bring your pet for Pet Day."

Everyone seemed to understand as they trooped through the gate to their parents. "Friday's Pet Day!" they told their parents. "Friday's Pet Day! Friday's Pet Day!"

Becky let out a big "Whew!" when the last of the Funners climbed into their parents' cars.

After they'd all waved goodbye, Becky turned to Tricia. "Why on earth did you say Friday was Pet Day without even asking us? Something like that could turn into a real nightmare. Remember when Blake Berenson brought his white mice for show and tell? It was Butterscotch, your very own cat, who nearly ate them!"

Tricia spread her arms in helplessness. "We only had seven Funners today, why else? We need to get them and their friends back here before things get worse!"

"Makes sense to me," Cara said. "We have to do something to at least keep the ones we've got. Mrs. Leonard told me the Teeners are having a play-care, too, and not charging as much as we are."

"You're kidding!" Becky said.

Cara shook her head. "I'm not. When Jess and Melanie come back from their trip, we might not even have a club left. Actually, I was glad when Tricia mentioned Pet Day. Anything to keep today's Funners coming and to bring the others back."

They all went back to the redwood table to clean up, discussing other ways to get more Funners to come.

"It wasn't our best Magic Carpet Ride ever," Cara remarked, "not after Melanie's Auntie Ying-Ying helped with our Chinese New Year Parade. But today's sure turned interesting when Pinky Royster disappeared. What happened with him?"

Tricia rolled her eyes. "He climbed over the fence into the Cooblers' yard."

"Over that fence?" Cara repeated. "I can't believe it!"

"I know, but he did," Tricia answered. "Mom didn't want to give the other Funners any ideas about climbing it. She called Mrs. Coobler, who told her. Anyhow, Pinky is there."

"He sure is a peculiar kid," Cara said. "Is he a Coobler relative or what?"

"He's homeless," Tricia answered. "Nobody knows how it happened, but he's homeless. Mrs. Coobler's church is helping him and other troubled kids. She's going to keep him at her house for a while to see if they want to be foster parents."

Cara's heart hurt for him. She might have a lot of troubles with Paige, and the club might be having trouble with the Teeners, but none of their problems were as bad as Pinky's. None of them were homeless.

"One thing about him," Tricia remarked, "he's a real somersaulter."

"You're right about that," Cara agreed. "He somersaulted into our lives, then somersaulted out." It was strange, but she almost felt as if he'd somersaulted into her heart. No sense in telling them he might have grabbed some raisins on his way out.

She added, "What scared me, I guess, is that if we lost a Funner—or if something else terrible happened, the club would be ruined for sure."

———

Finally the mess from Morning Fun for Kids was cleaned up, and Becky had to go out to the street, since her gram was going to pick her up.

"I'll walk you two out front," Tricia told them.

They strolled through the breezeway thoughtfully.

"You know, it's peculiar," Tricia said. "That verse keeps coming to me: 'And we know that all things work together for good to them that love God, to them who are the called according to his purpose.' "

"I wonder why," Becky said.

Tricia raised her reddish blond brows. "I think God wants to use it as a reminder. You know, to encourage us."

"I hope so," Becky said.

Cara didn't know what to say, since God had never sent a verse to her. It was hard to believe that He even *would*, though she guessed that He *could*. After all, you'd think God could do anything He wanted to do.

"The thing we have to remember," Tricia said, "is that God wants us to keep this club together and for us to stay friends. I think He wants us to reach out to others, and even be an example to Paige and her friends."

"That's the hard part," Cara said, "being friends with Paige. You know, I was just thinking that God doesn't ever send me verses, but I've been remembering from the youth group . . . *a gentle answer turns away wrath*. The only trouble is, I haven't been using it with Paige."

"It's a hard thing to do," Becky told her. "But we'll pray that God will give you the strength to do it."

Across the cul-de-sac, at the older Lins's house, the garage door went up, and their red Buick started out. That meant Melanie's Uncle Gwo-Jenn was driving—a far safer driver than her cousin, Connie Fender-Bender.

The garage door closed as the red Buick backed out of their driveway. As usual, Auntie Ying-Ying sat in the front passenger seat, and she saw them the moment they drove into the cul-de-sac. She let down her window and waved excitedly.

As the car pulled out onto La Crescenta, Auntie shouted, "Looks good for you job! Big job . . . take all of you! I let you know when for sure."

"Is it baby-sitting Silvee and William?" Tricia asked, meaning Melanie's younger sister and brother.

Auntie Ying-Ying shook her head hard. "No . . . this *big* job. Secret . . . very secret. Week and a half away. . . ." She grinned widely, and Uncle Gwo-Jenn just gave them his usual polite nod before they drove off down the street.

"The way things are going," Cara said, "we'll need a *big* job by then. A very big job!"

"Is my memory going?" Tricia asked. "Didn't she say almost the same thing before?"

Trying to remember, Cara said, "I think so, except now we know it's a secret and a week and a half away."

"Wonder what kind of a job it could be?" Becky asked.

"Maybe they're having another birthday party in their courtyard," Tricia guessed.

They looked at the front courtyard wall across the street. "The Great Wall of China," Melanie called it.

The white stucco wall stood toward the front between the two Lin houses. Three gray sea gulls in flight filled the right upper side, and a brass strip like a sunset curved over the lower section. A real willow tree stood near the wall, and a carpet of purple ice plant bloomed all the way out to the street. Behind the wall, you could see the second stories of the two white houses and their red-tiled roofs, and, between them, the red-tiled roof over the courtyard.

"Maybe it's going to be a party for co-workers from Dr. Lin's hospital," Tricia added. "They'd probably have a big crowd, and they'd want us to serve. Or it could be something for artists like Melanie's mother. Who knows what Auntie Ying-Ying might plan while Melanie and her parents are away?"

"Do you think Auntie Ying-Ying would make such a big deal of us just serving for a party?" Becky asked.

Cara shrugged. "I think she gets excited about most things. She's an enthusiastic person."

"I don't know," Becky said. "I have a feeling it's something bigger than a party."

"Well, we'd better not get too excited about it," Tricia warned. "We might be disappointed."

Just then, Becky's gram drove onto their street a block away. Becky remarked, "Gram is being so good about getting me around." She darted a look at the "For Sale" sign in front of her house. "I hope our move is going to be mostly okay."

"Me too," Cara agreed.

"What are you doing before the meeting?" Becky asked her.

"Maybe organizing my closet to see what I need for

school," Cara decided. "And maybe some reading."

Becky rolled her eyes. "You know, Tricia is the only TCCer with a baby-sitting job this afternoon?"

Cara nodded. "I know it! It's sure disappointing after having so many jobs at first. It seemed like our jobs would never stop." She drew a breath. "Well, see you."

Tricia called after her, "And we know that all things come together for good to those who love God and are called according to His purpose!"

It didn't make sense to her, Cara decided as she made her way toward her house. It didn't make much sense at all.

Dear Journal,

This afternoon I organized my clothes for school, even though there's almost a whole month to go. Now I'm sitting on the patio lounge in the warm afternoon sunshine.

When I returned from MFK, no one was home. I love the quiet—except for those phone calls for Paige. She's getting lots of them for Teener jobs, so far from no one I know. I don't like taking her messages, so I'm counting on our answering machine for a while. Gee—I hope Jess's answering machine is working today, since Dad put in a brand-new tape.

TCC had a quiet Morning Fun for Kids, except for that new boy—Pinky Royster—who disappeared during the Magic Carpet Ride. I've thought about him a lot, and about being homeless. I think it would mean being wet and cold, and hungry and dirty—and l-o-n-e-l-y. Thinking about it makes me glad for my family, even though we're not perfect. Not yet anyhow—ha!

But I'm feeling sad, too. The club was going so well! It's depressing now. Everything's slowed to a crawl. At least we have that clowning birthday party tomorrow afternoon.

What's killing me most is Paige stealing our TCC ideas and trying to ruin our club. It makes me furious. I know I'm supposed to forgive her and everything, but it's so hard to do. Tricia and Becky talk about God a lot, and tell me He's the only one who can help me love Paige . . . (and sometimes Mom, too!). I know I need help, and I'm trying to remember "A gentle answer turns away wrath." But it's not easy when you're mad!

"This meeting of the Twelve Candles Club shall now come to order," Becky said in Jess's bedroom-gym. Within minutes, the three of them were through the reports. Next, they discussed the sad state of the club's business. Unfortunately, it still included *no messages on the answering machine and the phone still not working.* This time Tricia offered to call the phone company from her house.

"Is there any new business?" Becky asked.

Tricia put up a hand. "I have an idea for the clown birthday party tomorrow afternoon. I was thinking about Jess being gone and no clown to do cartwheels and flips. It adds so much to the fun."

She hesitated. "What do you all think about inviting Pinky Royster to dress as a clown for the party and do somersaults?"

"Pinky Royster!" Cara exclaimed. "He's only five years old himself. The same age as the birthday girl."

"I know it," Tricia answered. "That's exactly what I thought when the idea hit. Than I asked Mom about it, and she called Mrs. Coobler just to toss out the idea before we discussed it. Well, Mrs. Coobler asked Pinky, just in case, and he liked it!"

"You mean he talks?" Becky asked.

Tricia laughed. "Or grins a lot!"

"Let's discuss it more," Becky suggested. "First of all, we don't have Jess's permission to use her clown outfit—"

"Actually we do," Cara interrupted. "I'd almost forgotten. She told me if we could find someone to take her place, they could wear it. But it would be huge on Pinky."

"Mom already considered that," Tricia said. "For one thing, Jess isn't all that tall, and we could put those thick bands on the legs and arms to hold up the extra fabric while Pinky wears it."

Cara shook her head. "It would still be huge on him, especially in the shoulders. Maybe we could rent a little clown outfit—"

"Too expensive," Tricia said. "You know, we might be able to find a small clown outfit through the theater companies in town. Mom would know who to call because she's always sewing outfits to help them. Hey, maybe Mom can just take some extra tucks in the outfit's shoulders."

She shook her head at herself. "Before we worry too much about that, what do you two think about Pinky doing it?"

"Would we pay him?" Cara asked.

"I think we should," Becky answered. "He probably needs the money more than we do."

Cara agreed right away, as did Tricia.

"One other thing," Tricia said. "The birthday party mom, Mrs. Merrill, sometimes attends the same church as Mrs. Coobler, so they know each other. That might be important. Maybe Pinky won't hold up for the entire party, and Mrs. Coobler will have to come get him."

"Or he might disappear over the fence, too," Cara added with concern.

"It's a risky idea, all right," Tricia said, "but I thought it was worth discussing. We should consider how Jess and Melanie might feel about it, too."

Becky pounded her hand on Jess's desk for attention. "Before we go any further, let's stop and have a vote."

She added in her presidential tone, "If it's agreeable with the birthday mom, Mrs. Merrill, how many in favor of inviting Pinky Royster to be a somersaulting clown at Victoria Merrill's birthday party?"

Cara raised her hand slowly, followed by Becky and then Tricia.

Becky asked, "Will someone make a motion?"

By the time Pinky being invited was moved, seconded, and passed, Cara felt good about it. At least it was better than always worrying about their phone troubles and the Teeners. Pinky would probably make the party more exciting and kids liked exciting parties.

Someone knocked at the door, and Cara made her way through the gym equipment to answer. When she opened the door, she was surprised to see Bryan Bennett.

"Mom sent me with the newspaper," he blurted. His eyes barely met Cara's, then he turned and ran. Probably he thought he'd get in trouble with Tricia for interrupting their meeting.

"Thanks," Cara shouted after him.

"Thanks, Bryan!" Tricia called out.

Cara carried the newspaper toward the twin beds corner. "Let's see what that editorial person wrote. I guess it should be on the letter-to-the-editor page."

She flipped through the paper and found the page. Surveying it, she finally huffed, "Well! It's in tiny print and at the very bottom of the page!"

Becky and Tricia looked over her shoulder as Cara read. "The Editorial Department normally checks the readers whose letters to the editor are printed. Unfortunately that wasn't the case in yesterday's letter titled *Workers Too Young?*, written by a T. L. Thompson. The writer gave no address nor phone number, which is required by this newspaper. We apologize for this oversight to Cara Hernandez and to the Twelve Candles Club."

"Well, that's something!" Tricia said.

"But not much," Becky added. "No one will even see it!"

That was exactly how Cara felt. "I don't think it will undo much of the damage that's been done."

No matter what happened, the club was still in trouble!

CHAPTER

6

Thursday, just after noon, Cara rode her bike down La Crescenta to Tricia's house. Her yellow polka-dotted clown suit and yellow yarn wig lay folded up in the plastic bag under her bike rack.

Clowning was one thing the Teeners weren't likely to copy. Tricia and Becky had taken clowning classes, and Cara doubted that Sandra Bassinger or Leigh Warrick ever had. Paige sure hadn't. Besides, Twelve Candles had great clown outfits, since Tricia's mother knew a lot about sewing costumes.

Cara's thoughts returned to last night when Paige had come home—exactly in time for dinner. Sitting down at the table, she'd raised her chin, as usual.

"Well," Mom had said, "how are the Teeners doing?"

For a change, they'd had a home-cooked dinner, and Paige had been cutting a meat ball. "The Teeners are doing just wonderful," she'd answered. "We can hardly keep up with all of the jobs. We're even doing a kids' birthday party Friday. It'll be the best ever given in Santa Rosita!"

Cara pressed her lips together angrily.

"Good," Mom replied. "You'll be able to buy whatever you might still need for school."

"And gas for your car," Dad added. "Actually, there's nothing as satisfying as earning your own money."

Paige darted a glance at Cara. "*Car-o-leena* doesn't seem to think so. She's jealous of the Teeners being so busy. Look at her, she's jealous-jealous-jealous!"

Am not! Cara was tempted to snap back. *I'm mad!* Next, she was tempted to ask, *Have you stolen more of the Twelve Candles Club jobs?* Instead, she was surprised to remember, *A gentle answer turns away wrath.*

It took an effort, but she made herself smile. "I think it's a great idea for you to work, too, Paige. Dad's right. It's nice to earn your own money."

Paige's blue eyes widened with surprise, then turned angry. "Well, aren't you being nice, *Señorita Car-o-leena*?"

Cara focused on piercing a tomato in her salad, and Dad told Paige, "I don't appreciate your mocking Cara in Spanish, and I'm sure she doesn't either. It's a sign of bigotry on your part, and bigotry happens to be out of style lately."

For a change, Mom didn't say a word.

"Let's all try to live as a happy family," Dad added.

Cara expected Paige to flounce from the table. But she must have been hungry—or feeling guilty—because she just looked furious and kept on eating. Right after dinner, she'd left for a baby-sitting job, and Cara had wondered how

Paige might treat the kids she sat for. Maybe she acted differently with them.

That had been last night. And this morning Paige had still been asleep when Cara went out to wash cars with Tricia. Most of TCC's car-washing usually took place Saturday mornings, but Mr. and Mrs. Llewellyn were in Israel, so they hadn't had to clean house for them this morning. Switching most of the car-washing would make Saturday easier with just three of them to do it.

At lunchtime, Paige had been gone.

Now Cara coasted up Tricia's driveway, beginning to feel more excited about their clowning birthday party. The Bennetts' garage door was open, so she rode in and parked her bike next to Tricia's, then grabbed the clown suit bag. Mrs. Bennett would probably be helping them with their makeup out on the redwood patio table.

Cara remembered to push the garage door button to close it against possible burglars or the Coobler boys fooling around.

"Hey-hey!" she called out as she hurried into the breezeway. It occurred to her again that she didn't feel nearly as shy as she did before the club began.

Lively calliope music with ump-pa-pa sounds floated through the patio speakers, setting the mood. Probably they'd take the tape to the party for background music, something that they'd done once before.

"Here comes Lello!" she announced as she hurried around the corner into the Bennetts' backyard. She'd taken Lello for her clown name because of her yellow polka-dotted clown suit and yellow wig—and little kids often called yellow "lello."

To her amazement, Pinky Royster stood by the patio table wearing a colorful polka-dotted clown outfit, and Mrs. Bennett was trying a shaggy red, blond, and black wig on his head.

Cara exclaimed to Pinky, "Whoa, look at you!"

He grinned widely over his white neck ruffles, and Mrs. Bennett remarked, "Doesn't he look perfect?"

"He does."

Mrs. Bennett eased the red-blond-and-black wig off Pinky's head. "Now we know the wig fits too, so let's start your clown makeup." The redwood table held the makeup case, a stand-up mirror, and pictures of clowns in full makeup. "Isn't Pinky going to be a great clown?"

"You know it!" Cara answered.

Mrs. Bennett tied a purple necktie around his neck. "We have a black top hat for him, too," she said. "With the rest of you clowns being girls, we thought it was best to make him look like a boy clown."

Tricia hurried out the patio door in her green polka-dotted clown suit, yellow wig in hand. She wore little bells on her wrists and ankles to fit her clown name, Jingles.

Behind her came Becky in her blue clown suit with white polka-dots. "Here's Beck-o!" she announced.

Their hair was pinned up, ready for makeup and wigs.

"We decided that Pinky's clown name is Somersaulter," Tricia said, nodding toward him. "He's going to blow up balloons, too. Doesn't he look terrific?"

"He sure does," Cara answered, wondering if Pinky would actually do what they asked. He could ruin the whole birthday party—which would help ruin the club. It was encouraging, though, to see him looking so happy.

Cara asked, "Where did Pinky's clown outfit come from?"

"From leftover pieces of all of yours!" Mrs. Bennett said with a laugh.

Sure enough, Pinky's sleeves were yellow with big white polka-dots like her own clown suit, Cara noticed. His pant legs were leftover green with white polka-dots, from Tricia's clown suit. The front was blue with white polka-dots like Becky's. And the back was from Jess's—red with white polka-dots. Melanie hadn't done any clowning yet.

"He's wearing yarn from our wigs, too," Tricia put in. "You might say Pinky is a little like all of us!"

Pinky kept right on grinning.

"Have you ever seen a circus or circus clowns?" Becky asked him.

He just grinned more widely.

Cara hoped so. Maybe he'd at least seen a clown on a TV in a store window. Or maybe he hadn't always been homeless and had actually been to a circus.

Mrs. Bennett began to smear the white glop on his face. "You're going to look wonderful, Pinky. Oops! I mean Somersaulter. Maybe you'll want to be a clown when you grow up. Clowns bring lots of happiness."

Cara guessed that he understood. In fact, he looked as if he were taking in a lot, but just wasn't ready to give anything out yet. She'd heard about people like that who turned out to be geniuses. "Pinky Royster, are you a genius?"

His grin edged sideways.

"Come on, girls, you have to get ready," Mrs. Bennett said urgently. "Mrs. Merrill wants you there before one o'clock so little Victoria can get used to you. Mrs. Coobler is going to help out in the kitchen. She'll drive you in her minivan."

"How about that!" Tricia remarked.

Cara felt a surge of relief. "It's a lot better than the time we rode to the first clown party on our bikes and every car on Ocean Avenue honked at us!"

They laughed at the memory.

"I'd better get dressed," Cara said.

"Up in my bedroom, as usual," Tricia told her.

Some minutes later, Cara hurried back outside in her yellow clown suit with the white polka-dots. Strange, how she felt like a different person as Lello the Clown. Once she wore her makeup, Lello wouldn't be the least bit shy!

Mrs. Bennett had almost finished making up Tricia and Becky. She stood waiting to help with their wigs while they put on their own big red foam-rubber noses.

Nearby, Pinky Royster admired himself in the mirror. His makeup was perfect: a big red smiley mouth, red circles on his cheeks, a red foam-rubber nose, thick dark eyebrows, and blue triangles above and below his blue eyes. The rest of them wore tennis shoes, but not Pinky. He was barefooted, as usual.

"An idea!" Cara exclaimed. "When Mrs. Merrill phoned about the birthday party, she mentioned a big barrel we could use for presents. I told her we usually give out presents by spinning the bottle, which she liked better. But I just thought how we could use that barrel. At the end of the party, we can hide Pinky in it and roll him out. Then we up-end it, and he jumps up and hands out our clown coloring pages."

She turned to Pinky. "Would you like to do that?"

He beamed, making his clown mouth smile even wider.

Tricia and Becky yelled, "Yeah, Pinky!!!! Yeah!!!!!"

He raced for the grass and turned a somersault.

"Yeah, Pinky!!!!!!" they all shouted again, making him turn another.

"Yelling 'Yeah!!!!' looks like the secret to success to get him somersaulting," Cara said. She sat down at the table and let Mrs. Bennett slather the white glop on her face. Next came the green triangles under and above her eyes, then big red circles on her cheeks and wide smiling mouth. Last, she put on the red foam-rubber nose.

Everyone was ready when Mrs. Coobler arrived in the backyard. She was plump and pleasant, and she looked at them in amazement. "Why, I feel like I've arrived at the circus! There's even circus music!"

"Yipes, we don't dare forget that tape," Tricia said. "Also our party gifts and list."

Before long, they were climbing into Mrs. Coobler's red minivan. Luckily, the neighbors weren't out. Tricia and Becky headed for the backseat, setting the face-painting kit between them, so Cara sat in the middle seat section. Grinning, Pinky settled behind her, then plopped his black top hat on his head. As the club secretary, Cara had the circus music tape, the clown coloring pages gift, and the things-to-do list, and Tricia suggested, "Why don't you read the list, Cara, so Pinky will know what we're doing, too."

Cara drew a breath, wondering if he'd even understand it.

"1. Face-painting as kids arrive,

"2. Hokey-Pokey,

"3. Sing 'Old MacDonald Had a Farm,' 'Row, Row,

Row Your Boat,' and other little kid songs,

"4. Comedy (balloon, elastic, and vegetable-stand skits),

"5. Balloon animals,

"6. Birthday present circle,

"7. Our gifts for kids. Pinky gives them from barrel."

She told Pinky, "Actually, our clown gifts are clown coloring pages with our club name and phone number." She wasn't sure if he understood, but he was looking at her list again. "Hey, can you read?"

Grinning, he raised his chin as if to say that's-for-me-to-know-and-for-you-to-find-out.

She spoke to him softly so the others couldn't hear. "I think maybe you swiped some raisin packs at Tricia's yesterday. Make sure you don't swipe anything at this party. You could get all of us in trouble."

His pale blue eyes darted past her, and he pressed his lips together stubbornly.

She'd have to watch him during the party. "We're trusting you, Pinky. We're trusting you a lot . . . and we've already got lots of trouble! Besides, we're going to give you a fourth of our money."

A passing driver honked his car horn at them, and everyone except Pinky gave the driver a big clown wave. Cara thought he must be thinking over what she'd told him.

Before they turned onto the Merrills' street, Tricia said from the backseat, "Time for prayer."

Cara had scarcely closed her eyes before Tricia prayed, thanking God for giving them creativity, and asking His blessing on their work at the birthday party.

"Amen!" Becky echoed when Tricia finished.

"Amen," Cara added.

She glanced at Pinky and saw he was opening his eyes, too. Maybe he was a believer or a "seeker after God," as Tricia and Becky called it. Whatever, he looked as if he had listened to the prayer.

Yellow balloons bobbed on the mailbox in front of the Merrills' one-story white house. Two white pillars stood near the front door, making the house unusual for Santa Rosita. Mrs. Coobler parked the minivan, and after everyone got out, Cara hung back to question Mrs. Coobler about Pinky. Not that she'd tell about his possibly swiping raisins. Maybe homeless kids took food any chance they got!

"Could you tell me about Pinky?"

Mrs. Coobler's round face turned serious. "You must mean his not talking. Actually, no one knows much about him except that he was homeless for a while. Before he came here, he lived for a year in a temporary foster home with twelve older kids, so he didn't have to talk. He pointed, and they got him whatever he wanted. I think this clowning will be great fun for him."

"I hope so," Cara replied. "Is he going to stay here or is his living with you temporary, too?"

Mrs. Coobler shook her head with concern. "We don't know yet. We're waiting to see how it goes. I felt so strongly led to bring him to Morning Fun for Kids this morning. I thought maybe something would happen there to make him talk—"

"Come on, Cara!" Tricia yelled from the gate.

"I . . . I have to go!" Cara said to Mrs. Coobler. She ran to join Tricia and Becky, then they burst into the backyard singing, "Happy birthday to you! Happy birthday to you!

Happy birthday, dear Victoria . . ."

Victoria Merrill, a blond girl in a fluffy pink dress, was so surprised that her blue eyes nearly burst from her head.

"It's the Polka-dot Clowns here for your birthday," her mother said. "This is Jingles and Lello and Beck-o. They've even brought a little clown with them."

Usually Jess turned cartwheels right now to keep the birthday boy or girl from being too scared. But Jess wasn't here—and Victoria Merrill definitely looked frightened!"

"Somersault!" Becky-Beck-o yelled, but Pinky didn't budge.

Victoria looked ready to turn one herself, but her mother warned, "Not you, Victoria! Not in that new dress!"

"Yeah, Pinky!!!" Cara-Lello called out, then Becky-Beck-o and Tricia-Jingles joined in. "Yeah, Pinky!!! Yeah, Pinky!!!"

Pinky's clown mouth widened in a huge smile, and he took off somersaulting around the yard, his bare feet flying. Luckily the elastic band under his wig held it on.

Victoria clapped her hands. "Yeah, Pinky!!!!"

"So much for calling him Somersault!" Cara remarked.

After he'd somersaulted around the yard, Tricia-Jingles yelled, "That's enough, Pinky. You can do more later."

"We need you to blow up balloons now, Pinky!" Cara called out behind him.

That brought him to a stop.

She handed him balloons they'd brought, and once the balloon was in the balloon-blowing device, Pinky worked the pump to blow it up. He worked along happily while Victoria Merrill watched. She seemed to prefer a clown her own size to the rest of them.

"Pinky's five years old, like you," Cara-Lello told her. "He's a five-year-old clown."

Victoria and Pinky eyed each other with interest. For Pinky, it looked like love at first sight.

After a moment, Victoria asked, "Doesn't he talk?"

Cara-Lello's throat squeezed shut. If she said Pinky didn't talk, maybe it would discourage him. If she said he talked, it'd be lying, since it appeared that he didn't.

Tricia-Jingles and Becky-Beck-o looked just as puzzled. Suddenly car doors slammed out front.

"Here come your guests!" Mrs. Merrill told Victoria.

Cara-Lello thought to ask her the location of the barrel. "On the other side of the garage," Mrs. Merrill answered. "We hosed it out for your plan."

"I'll put our clown gifts there now." Cara rushed off around the garage and found the barrel. It was sturdy and dry now. She stuck the envelope with clown coloring pages under it.

When she returned to the patio, three little girls were arriving in the backyard, birthday presents in hand.

Jingles did a jingly dance for them, the bells on her wrists and ankles jingling. "I'm Jingles, the Clown. May I take your birthday gifts for Victoria to the birthday table?"

Wide-eyed at the clowns, the girls gave up their presents wordlessly. Everyone was quiet, painfully quiet.

Jess would have done flips to liven things up, Cara thought. She shouted, "Yeah, Pinky!!!!"

Pinky set down the balloons, one sputtering out air. He raced to the grass and began to somersault.

Cara-Lello's eyes met Becky-Beck-o's, and they both laughed aloud. On the patio, the circus tape added to the fun with its lively calliope music.

When Pinky stopped, Tricia-Jingles asked the girls, "May we clowns paint your faces? We can paint hearts, rainbows, spiders, and shooting stars."

"A rainbow!" one girl said.

"Hearts!" piped another.

As more girls arrived, Cara felt like the party would be a success, thanks to Pinky's help. Mrs. Merrill talked to parents and Mrs. Coobler answered phone calls while Cara-Lello greeted the newcomers and took their gifts to the birthday table. Pinky did more somersaults, and Becky-Beck-o and Tricia-Jingles painted the new arrivals' faces. When all fifteen guests had arrived, the giggling grew louder and louder.

Tricia-Jingles jingled her wrist bells over their heads. "And now, if everyone will form a circle, the Polka-dot Clowns will lead you in dancing the world-famous *Hokey-Pokey*.

Cara grabbed the hands of two girls, who stared uneasily at her. "Jingles and the other Polka-Dot clowns will show us how to do the Hokey-Pokey."

"All right, let's do it!" Tricia-Jingles called out. "You put your right foot in, you put your right foot out. . . ."

After three rounds of the Hokey-Pokey, the kids were bright-eyed and giggling.

Next, they all sat cross-legged on the patio and sang "Old MacDonald Had a Farm" and a few other kid songs.

After that came Tricia-Jingle's balloon and telephone jokes, which always brought laughs. The telephone joke was usually a favorite, and Cara-Lello brought Tricia-Jingles a long white piece of elastic with a red pompom tied to each end.

"Look," Jingles said. "I have a new invention. Lello, you hold that end, and I'll hold this end. Now, let's stretch this invention as far as it will go."

When the elastic was stretched to its limit, Jingles added, "Now, I'll say, 'Ring, ring, ring—I have a phone call for you.' Then you say, 'Let me have it.' "

Lello eyed her red pompom from every direction, then nodded happily.

Jingles yelled, "Ring, ring, ring!" Putting her red pompom to her ear, she said, "I have a phone call for you!"

Lello smiled, looking simple-minded. "I wonder if it's my Aunt Agnes from Altoona?"

"No, no, no!" Jingles answered. "When I say, 'I have a phone call for you,' you say, 'Let me have it.' Now let's try again. Ready?"

Lello nodded.

Jingles grinned mischievously at the kids, then turned to Lello. "Ring, ring, ring!" She put the red pompom to her ear and said, "I have a phone call for you."

Lello jumped excitedly. "I wonder if it's my cousin, calling to ask me to a ball game!"

"NO! NO! NO!" Jingles yelled impatiently. "When I say, 'I have a phone call for you,' you say, 'Let me have it.' " She shook her head. "Are you ready?"

Lello shrugged, then answered, "Ready."

"Ring, ring—"

"WAIT!" Lello interrupted. "What do I say?"

Jingles bellowed, *Let me have it!*

Lello let go of the elastic band, knocking Jingles down

with the pompom, and, as usual, the kids roared with laughter.

Next came a funny one called the Vegetable Stand, then before long, it was time to sing "Happy Birthday."

As everyone sang, Victoria beamed and Pinky watched her with interest. He looked almost as if he wanted to sing along with them, too.

At last, Cara, Becky, and Tricia handed around dishes of ice cream and cake.

After they'd eaten, Cara-Lello and Becky-Beck-o seated the girls in a circle, and Tricia-Jingles brought out a plastic bottle with bells on it.

"Here's the very best part!" Tricia-Jingles exclaimed. "I spin this jingly bottle, and whoever it points to gives their present to Victoria."

The girls bounced and giggled, and Pinky sat on the edge of the patio, watching eagerly. Everything was going well, Cara thought. The Teeners couldn't do a better party. Of course, this one wasn't over.

When there were three gifts left to give, Cara-Lello led Pinky to the other side of the garage. She told him, "We'd like you to get in the barrel, then I'll roll it over to the party. When I set the barrel up, you pop out with the clown coloring pages. You want to do it?"

Pinky looked confused or maybe he didn't want to do it.

As she rolled the barrel around to its side, she tried to explain in another way. "When the barrel stands up, you pop up with the clown coloring pages."

She gave him the pages, and he eyed them curiously. Becky had drawn a coloring picture of four clowns playing tricks on each other, then photocopied it. On the bottom, it said, "THE POLKA-DOT CLOWNS—Birthday Parties, Picnics, and Programs of all kinds!" Below that, she'd printed Jess's phone number, which Cara desperately hoped was working again.

Pinky must have changed his mind because he climbed into the barrel and braced himself, pleased at the adventure.

"Hold on!" Cara-Lello told him. "Here we go!"

She rolled the barrel around into the backyard, and Becky-Beck-o hurried over to help. Tricia-Jingles started the girls singing another chorus of "Happy Birthday."

At the end of the song, Cara-Lello and Becky-Beck-o righted the barrel. "Now!" Cara whispered to Pinky.

He popped out, the clown coloring papers in hand. Pinky opened his big red smiley mouth. "Happy birthday!" he yelled to Victoria. "Happy birthday!!!!"

In awe, Mrs. Coobler called out, "Praise God!"

Cara's heart leapt with excitement. Tricia had prayed that God would bless the birthday party—and Pinky had spoken! Cara felt almost like calling out a "Praise God!" herself. It was so perfect.

At this moment, everything seemed brighter. It seemed dumb to think about it this way—but if God could help Pinky talk, maybe God could also fix the TCC phone problems, make up for that horrible letter-to-the-editor, and even do something about that nasty half sister of hers, Paige, and her Teeners!

CHAPTER

7

The next morning, everyone in Cara's family rose early for breakfast. Cara sat at the round oak dining area table because Mom didn't like them to eat meals from the bar stools at the white-tiled kitchen counter.

Lately Mom had been saying, "Let's eat like *civilized people* at a table." Now she and Dad came to sit down with Cara at the dining table.

Even Paige was up early for breakfast. In fact, she was helping herself to a bowl of cereal in the kitchen. This morning, she wore a look-at-me red tank top and shorts.

For an instant, Cara wondered if she should tell her half sister that as a blond she'd look a lot better in blue than red, but what good would it do? Paige would snap back something mean at her. So much for the youth pastor saying, "Truth always wins out."

Cara decided that she felt good about her jean cut-offs

and old blue Tee. There was no sense in wearing new clothes for Morning Fun for Kids, especially on Pet Day! She'd already decided not to take Angora. There'd probably be dogs and other cats . . . and who knew what other kinds of animals.

Dad remarked to Paige, "It's unusual to see you up so early. The Teeners must have another job this morning."

"As a matter of fact, we do," Paige answered snootily from the kitchen. "Twelve Candles isn't the only club in Santa Rosita that can do a morning play-care."

"You've copied us there, too! Wasn't it bad enough stealing Mrs. O'Lone's work from us? It serves you right, sloshing window-washing water all over yourself and your so-called friends! I'll bet you got water on the O'Lones' inside carpet, and ruined your friends' hair—"

"Cara!" Mom interrupted. "I will say, you do have your father's Latino temper."

Cara's eyes met Dad's, and she could see he was trying to hold his temper, too. After a moment, he turned to Paige. "What's this about sloshing water all over?"

"Never mind!" she snapped.

"Let's not pick on Paige," Mom said.

Cara could scarcely believe how Mom forever defended Paige. It seemed that the two of them always teamed up against Dad and her! But to be fair, though, Dad usually defended her, Cara thought. Maybe her parents didn't know they were always against each other, but it sure made family life hard. Sadly, it was the same at Flick's Video where Mom thought almost any kind of video was fine for customers to see. She'd say, "If people don't see videos that are so-called 'bad,' how can they recognize 'good'?"

Dad had answered, "Bad videos drag people down farther and farther . . . down so far they don't even know that good exists! If we don't stand up for decency at Flicks, we soon won't stand for anything, no matter how bad it is. I say it's time to stand up for family values."

Cara tended to agree with Dad.

Now he asked her, "Is Jess's phone and answering machine working?"

"I hope so."

"What do you mean, 'I hope so'?!" Mom asked.

Actually it was an embarrassing subject—and now she'd have to explain it, Cara thought. "The truth is I was so tired after the birthday party that I lay down on my bed for a few minutes. Well . . . I slept until after midnight! You were all in bed, so I just had a glass of milk and went back to bed, then I slept until this morning."

Mom blinked with surprise. "When we came home, I decided you needed to sleep. I had no idea you'd been in bed since afternoon!"

"What about your club meeting?" Dad asked. "Don't you have Jess's key?"

Cara nodded. "We were all so tired, we'd already decided to skip the meeting. I was just supposed to go over for phone messages—"

"You all skipped the meeting?" Mom asked.

Cara nodded again. "Not very smart, was it? I guess we were tired from working and . . . tired of phone trouble. It was such a good birthday party, we just wanted to think about that. Anyhow, we didn't have the meeting."

"Sounds bad to me," Mom remarked.

Cara felt like crawling under the table and was glad her father made no response.

Paige carried her glass of orange juice and bowl of cereal on a tray to the table. She boasted, "*We* had fifteen kids for Teener Play-Care last time. How many did *you* have?"

"Enough," Cara said. At least her answer was kinder than a snappy "None of your business!" No way would she tell Paige they'd only had six Funners—and that counted one free brother and two free sisters.

She was curious about where they had Teener Play-Care but decided not to ask. Instead, she ate her granola faster to get away from the table.

"Cara, you are gobbling your cereal," Mom said. "It's best to eat more slowly."

"Sorry," Cara replied.

Fortunately, there was only milk on the bottom of her white cereal bowl now. She kept her eyes on the tiny blue flowers around its rim and mentally counted, *One-two-three-four-five*, between spoonsful.

Paige had settled on her chair as if she were Miss Precious Princess. "I hear money was stolen at Mrs. Merrill's house during your clowning birthday party."

Stolen?! Cara's mind echoed.

"You don't have to pretend to be so surprised," Paige said. "Everyone already knows it."

Pinky! Cara thought. She'd already suspected him of swiping raisins at Morning Fun for Kids that first morning. She tried to calm herself. "What do you mean 'everyone' knows?"

Paige raised her chin and replied with a breezy, "Just

everyone in Santa Rosita, California, and maybe the whole world beyond."

Dad's voice was kind. "Do you know anything about money being stolen, Cara?"

"I know *I* didn't steal money, or anything else for that matter. And I'm sure that Tricia and Becky didn't either. We aren't thieves, like some people I know."

"Well!" Paige huffed.

"Now, Cara," Mom warned. "You know that Paige returned the money she borrowed from your closet."

"Borrowed!" Cara exclaimed. "She snuck into my room without my permission and took all of my money!"

Mom spoke soothingly. "Paige returned some of her new school clothes to pay you back. It couldn't have been easy for her to return them to the stores."

Cara's eyes slid past her half sister's gaze. "I guess not. Well . . . may I be excused from the table?"

"Apologize to Paige first," Mom said.

Cara clenched her fists, trying to think of what to say. Finally she managed, "I'm sorry I called you a thief." She didn't look Paige in the eye, but Paige wasn't looking her in the eye, either. In fact, she was eating as if she didn't have a concern in the world.

Cara rose from the table. "I'm . . . I'm sorry. Excuse me from the table, please." She wished she were truly sorry and that she hadn't brought up the truth. Here was another example of truth *not* winning out!

"Let's all try to have a good day," Dad said.

It was definitely not off to a good start, Cara thought. How hard it was to "turn away wrath," especially when that wrath was eating through you!

Paige asked, "What are you kiddos doing this morning for Morning Fun for Kids?"

"No way would I tell you!" Cara retorted. "I can't believe you'd have the nerve to even ask me about it!"

"Cara!" Mom warned.

Cara gathered up her empty juice glass and cereal bowl, knowing that her half sister watched from under her lashes. If Paige could arrange it, she'd ruin TCC. As for money disappearing at the Merrills' house, Paige was probably just plain lying, but they'd have to find out!

Just before nine o'clock, as Cara rode her bike up the Bennetts' driveway, Paige drove by and honked her horn. Cara tried to ignore her. Probably Paige would be late for Teeners' Play-Care, but she was always late for everything anyhow—and so were her friends.

The MORNING FUN FOR KIDS sign was already taped to the Bennetts' gate, and Cara parked her bike in the garage. Rushing out the side garage door over to the patio, she glanced toward the Cooblers' house and was glad that the Coobler boys weren't hanging over the fence. Nor was Pinky. Maybe it would be a good day after all.

"Hey-hey, Cara!" Tricia called out.

Cara smiled a little, even though she knew she'd have to ask about Pinky stealing money. She managed a cheerful, "You're sounding like Bear, the youth pastor."

"Another pet for Pet Day . . . meaning 'Bear' as in 'black bear' or 'brown bear' or 'polar bear,' " Becky joked. "Maybe we should have asked him to pray for Pet Day!"

"Maybe," Cara agreed. "You'll notice that I did *not* bring Angora with me."

"Amanda made us bring Lass," Becky answered. She rolled her blue eyes at their very old collie, who was already asleep in the sunshine at the edge of the patio.

"Mom says Chessie and Butterscotch are staying inside this morning," Tricia told them. "She figures we don't need another dog or cat to add to the excitement."

Cara sat down at the patio table with them. "Is it . . . is it true that money was stolen from the Merrills' during Victoria's birthday party?"

Becky nodded. "It's true, all right. Only a few quarters and pennies. But it was definitely stolen."

Cara drew a breath. "I guess I should tell you. I thought I saw Pinky swipe packs of raisins the last time he was here. On the way to Merrills', I warned him not to do anything like that again. Of course, he didn't answer."

"He did go in to use the bathroom," Becky said.

"I didn't notice," Cara answered. "That would have been his chance to take the money."

She glanced at the Cooblers' fence. Still no one there. "Wouldn't it be awful if he did steal the money? I mean after finally talking at the party!"

"Worse than awful!" Tricia replied. "On top of that, he hasn't done any more talking. It's a good thing Mrs. Coobler was at the party to hear him say 'Happy Birthday.'"

"At least we all heard that," Cara said.

"About the money," Becky put in, "we were in charge of the party. We brought him and we're responsible."

Tricia asked, "Who'll ask Pinky if he stole the money?"

Her throat was squeezing shut, but Cara said, "I guess

I should. I've spent the most time with him."

"You're on," Becky told her. "Thanks!"

"Someone has to ask him," Cara answered, half to herself. She hoped they wouldn't ask her about getting answering machine messages yesterday. It'd be too embarrassing to admit she'd slept instead. Besides, then they'd know she was going to ask Pinky partly to make up for sleeping through her responsibility.

Luckily, car doors slammed out front, and Funners began to arrive. Maybe Tricia and Becky would forget to ask about yesterday's answering machine messages.

Before long, the first four Funners wore their name tags and were getting out the Magic Carpet. No more arrived. All summer they'd begged for Pet Day, and now only s-e-v-e-n Funners had come for it, including Pinky. S-e-v-e-n—plus their pets, of course.

Craig Leonard's green and yellow parrot, named Alexa-Laura, stood on his shoulder looking about. "He talks a lot," Craig explained, "but not until he gets to know you. He's a little shy at first."

Exactly how she often felt, Cara thought, watching the bird. He jerked his head from side to side, his eyes huge, taking in everything.

Pinky Royster wasn't talking, either. At first it looked like his pet must be invisible, but he held his bib overalls' right pocket shut. He wasn't somersaulting, either, probably so he wouldn't squash whatever was in his pocket.

"Is whatever you put in your pocket snakey or mousey?" Cara asked, more worried about that now than about stolen money.

Pinky shook his head and grinned a little.

Everyone was watching him when a loud *Rrrrrrrrrivet!* erupted from his pocket. *Rrrrrivet! Rrrrivet! Rrrrrivet!*

"A frog!" the Funners yelled. "A frog! A frog! A frog!"

"And it sounds like a real one!" Becky added.

Pinky still wasn't talking, and it looked as if he didn't plan to show them his pet, either.

Suddenly Sam Miller's terrier dog, Whitey, yipped and began to run in big circles around the yard. Sam held tightly to Whitey's leash, so he took off too, running in circles after Whitey. Oddly enough, Whitey looked more green than white.

"He looks like Greeny!" Craig Leonard yelled.

"He's usually white," Sam answered as he ran. "He rolled outside on the grass right after his clipping and bath."

"Are you saying the grass turned his coat green?!" Cara asked with disbelief. "Come on!"

"That's why!" Sam replied, heading behind his greenish Whitey for the swing set. "Heel, Whitey! Heel!"

But Whitey wouldn't heel.

Sally Lowe, who was five years old, had brought her hamster, Hambone. Small, tan, and furry, he was nestled inside a shoebox with holes poked in it.

"A hamster's a dumb pet," Craig Leonard told her.

"Is not!" Sally replied indignantly. She squatted down, reached inside the shoebox, and petted Hambone.

"Now, now . . . you Funners!" Tricia warned. "Let's get out our Magic Carpet."

From the corner of her eye, Cara saw something greener than Whitey edging out of Pinky Royster's pocket. Suddenly it fell to the ground and jumped away wildly. *"Rrrrrrrrivet! Rrrrrrrrivet! Rrrrrrrrivet!"*

"A frog!" everyone shouted. "See, it's a frog like we thought!"

Pinky raced after the frog, trying to grab it, but it jumped wildly, zigging and zagging its way to the patio. The frog jumped right onto Becky's sleeping dog, Lass, and the old collie rose up with a loud bark.

Alerted, the Bennetts' golden retriever, Chessie, barked back, burst through the screen door, and ran toward the crazily hopping frog. Next, Butterscotch, the Bennetts' cat, raced through the hole in the screen and joined the chase. Lass and Chessie ran in circles around the lawn, barking excitedly, and the wacko frog jumped higher and farther, croaking, "Rrrriiirivet! Rrrrrrrrivet! Rrrrrrrrrivet!"

Suddenly, Butterscotch took a left turn and pounced near the shoebox. Poor Hambone wriggled quickly over the side of the box, and out into the grass.

"Hambone!!!" Sally Lowe shrieked, and she and Cara dove into the grass and crawled after him on all fours. "Keep that cat away from Hambone!" Sally cried. "Hambone! Oh, Hammy!"

Craig's parrot started jerking his head from side to side, disturbed by the racket. Suddenly, he flapped his green and red wings and flew with a "Whirrr!" from Craig's shoulder high up into the California pepper tree. He landed on a limb near the tree house. "Can't you be quiet? Can't you be quiet?" the bird squawked. "Awwwk! Awwwk! Can't you be quiet?"

Butterscotch leapt at Hambone—just as Cara scooped up the hamster in her hands. "Whewwwwwwwwwww!" she breathed, whirling away from the cat.

Tricia grabbed Butterscotch by the scruff of her neck

and hauled her up, shouting, "Who let you out here, Butterscotch?"

"Rrrrrrivet!" the frog croaked from somewhere under the sandbox. "Rrrrrrivet! Rrrrrrrivet! Rrrrrrivet!"

Lass, Chessie, and Whitey stood barking at the sandbox.

"Be nice!" Pinky Royster warned the dogs. He wagged a finger at them. "Be nice to Rivet!" He reached under the sandbox and pulled his green frog out from underneath. He planted a fast kiss on Rivet's nose and carefully placed him back into his pocket, then buttoned it shut.

Checking out the commotion, the Coobler boys peered over the fence. They shouted, "Pinky talks! Pinky talks!"

Suddenly, Alex-a-Laura dove down from the tree, straight at them, and the boys' faces disappeared from the top of the fence. Next came the sound of running footsteps, and all the Funners heard the Cooblers' back door slam shut with a bang.

The parrot flew back to his tree perch and squawked once more at the Funners, "Can't you be quiet? Can't you be quiet?"

Relieved, everyone roared with laughter.

When they quieted, and the pets were safely "corralled," Tricia called out, "Time for our Magic Carpet Ride!"

Today, the Funners rode the raggedy brown rug on an imaginary ride to the zoo. Meanwhile, Cara tried to coax Alex-a-Laura down from the tree, and grew more and more frantic. What if the parrot flew away?

All through crafts and snacks and the other activities, she tried to talk the bird down. "Come on, Alex-a-Laura, come on down, please." She approached the tree step by step, but every time she came too near, Alex-a-Laura raised his wings for flight. Little by little, Cara had edged a bit closer.

Suddenly Alex-a-Laura raised his wings and let out an angry, "Aaawk! Aaawk! Aaawk! Aaawk! Aaawk!"

"Calm down, bird. Calm down," Cara said, backing off. What would Mrs. Leonard say if the parrot flew away!

In the midst of the bird coaxing, she heard Tricia announce, "Next week is 'M-y-s-t-e-r-y P-l-a-y W-e-e-k.' We'll have an exciting m-y-s-t-e-r-y p-l-a-y all three days, and y-o-u can be in it. B-e s-u-r-e to tell your friends. We'll make c-o-s-t-u-m-e-s and have l-o-t-s of f-u-n."

They'd discussed "Mystery Play Week" several weeks ago, and it seemed like a good idea for next week, Cara thought. Anything to get more Funners to Morning Fun for Kids—and to *not* lose the ones attending today! And now to get Alex-a-Laura down from the tree! "Here, Alex-a-Laura . . . here's some graham cracker crumbs for you!"

The parrot raised his head in disdain.

When the parents arrived to pick up the Funners, Mrs. Leonard laughed to see their parrot in the tree. She made a clucking sound with her tongue, and Alex-a-Laura flew down onto her shoulder.

The Funners applauded, and the parrot asked, "Can't you be quiet? Can't you be quiet?"

Everyone laughed again, even Pinky.

Cara rolled her eyes. Thank goodness the bird hadn't flown off. Everyone in Santa Rosita would know that the TCC had let a family pet get away.

All she could think was, *I hope the Teeners' Play-Care has ten thousand times more trouble than the TCC!* Maybe she should have told Paige that today was Pet Day. After all, if the Teeners had fifteen kids with pets, it could be the nightmare of nightmares.

As the Funners left, they beamed and chattered to their parents about the morning. After Cara closed the front gate, she and Tricia and Becky picked up raisin boxes, apple juice cups, and globs of graham crackers from the sandbox, grass, patio, and everywhere else.

"All in all," Cara said, "I suppose Pet Day was a great success for the Funners . . . if not for us."

"Wildly successful," Becky agreed. Suddenly she slapped her mouth. "I almost forgot, the phone company told me Jess's phone is fixed. They said they'd had other complaints on it."

"That's great!" Cara said. "I'll stop at Jess's for messages. I have the key with me." Waiting for them to ask if she'd gotten last night's messages, she picked up a half-empty box of raisins from the grass.

Neither Becky nor Tricia asked. With so much going on in each of their lives, they'd probably forgotten.

"By the way," Cara began, "Paige told me that Teeners' Play-Care had fifteen kids Wednesday morning."

"Fifteen kids! No wonder our attendance is way down!" Tricia exclaimed. "And they're charging less! Let's discuss lowering our prices at the meeting." She turned to Cara. "Did you ask Pinky about the money?"

Cara felt heat rush to her cheeks. "In the middle of the pet chaos, I just plain forgot. I'll do it, though."

When the cleanup was finished, Tricia wiped her brow dramatically. "What we need is a vacation away from all of this craziness. A wonderful vacation somewhere else."

"Ha, are you kidding?" Becky asked. "The only vacation

we'll get from Morning Fun for Kids is going back to school next month. It'd be nice, though, to have a vacation."

"Maybe having this Club El Wacko is our vacation," Cara said.

Tricia gave a laugh. "A working vacation!"

"But fun, too," Becky said. "Maybe that's the way God planned this summer for us."

"Maybe," Tricia answered, "but look at Jess and Melanie off in Israel. Hey, just three days until they're back! We'd better get more jobs—lots of jobs—before then."

"You know it," Cara agreed.

On the way home on her bike, she noticed that Paige's red Thunderbird was already in the driveway. Strange that she'd get home so quickly, but maybe the Teeners didn't bother to clean up after their kids.

Cara rode up the driveway to Jess's house. No cars in the driveway . . . no newspapers or packages out front. She unlocked Jess's door and started in toward the desk, expecting to see the answering light blinking madly again.

Nothing blinked. . . . Nothing!

The answering machine was missing!

Jess's brothers wouldn't bother with it; they *never* came into the room. But how could someone else get in?

She inspected the room.

No broken windows . . . nothing disturbed.

Tumbles gave a yip in the backyard, and Cara hurried to the back window. She glanced through the back mini-blind, then knocked on the window at him. He wagged his brown tail and yipped happily. Everything was fine in his doggy yard.

Who was here? she wanted to ask him. *Who's making all the trouble?*

Something told her it was Paige and the Teeners.

But how?

CHAPTER

8

Cara locked Jess's door behind her, then hurried down the McColls' driveway. At her own house, Paige's red Thunderbird still stood in the driveway, but now Paige was in it. The car started with a roar and rock music boomed through the open window.

Cara raced across the street and shouted, "Did you steal Jess's answering machine?!"

"Are you kidding?" Paige asked. "If you'll excuse me, I have a big sitting job." With that, she backed out, tires squealing, and drove off.

A big baby-sitting job?

Cara wondered what it might be. Probably the Teeners stealing more TCC customers! She trudged to her front door, unlocked it, and started toward the kitchen.

First, she'd better call Dad about the missing answering machine. Next, she'd call Tricia and Becky. No. Becky was shopping for curtains and wallpaper with her gram, and Tricia was baby-sitting. They'd have to hear this bit of bad news at this afternoon's TCC meeting.

Just as she stepped through the kitchen archway, the phone rang. Probably a customer for the Teeners, Cara thought, then answered it anyhow. "Hello?"

"Is this Paige Larson?" an irate woman asked.

"No, I'm sorry. She's out."

"Well," the woman huffed, "you can tell her that Mrs. Kensington will no longer bring her children to Teener Play-Care! I'm never again paying for baby-sitters to ignore my children! There's no 'play' to it."

A thought flashed to Cara's mind: *Tell her about TCC!*

But the woman had already hung up.

Well was right! Cara thought. It sounded as if the Teeners were far from perfect, even if they charged less money.

She dialed the number for Flicks. Luckily Dad answered. "Now Jess's answering machine is missing!" Cara said. "I was just in Jess's room and it's missing!"

"Was anything else disturbed?" he asked.

"No . . . nothing that I noticed. And I checked things out, too."

After a moment, Dad said, "Maybe one of Jess's brothers took the answering machine to be repaired since there's been so much trouble with it and the phone. Garner strikes me as a responsible type. Let's wait until they get home tonight before we get involved with it. Answering machines are no longer so expensive. I doubt they're still a popular item for burglars to take."

Cara blurted, "I think maybe Paige did it!"

"How could she get into the room?" Dad asked.

"I don't know how. I'm careful to keep the key with me since we've had so much trouble."

"Did you keep the key with you before the trouble began?" Dad asked.

Thinking it over, Cara answered, "I had it hidden in my room then." It occurred to her that she'd had her money hidden, and Paige had found it.

Dad repeated, "I'm hoping the McColl boys took the machine to have it fixed."

"Maybe they did."

When they hung up, she felt somewhat reassured.

She opened the refrigerator and looked over the bread, cheese, and lunchmeat when the phone rang again. She closed the refrigerator.

"Cara?" a familiar voice asked.

What now?! "Yes. . . ."

"This is Mrs. Coobler. I have to get the older boys off to camp for two weeks, and—" She lowered her voice. "Pinky seems afraid that I'll send him away, too. I was wondering if you could sit with him from two until about five o'clock."

"I'd really like to, but I have our daily TCC meeting at four-thirty—"

"Could you take Pinky with you?" Mrs. Coobler asked. "He might not say much, but he seems so fond of you."

Cara recalled that Becky had brought her little sister Amanda a time or two. "Yes, I guess it'd be all right. I wouldn't be able to really play with him at the meeting. He'd have to just sit there."

"That's fine. I'll send along crayons and a new coloring book. And could you sit him at your house instead of ours before the meeting? Our house is going to be sprayed for ants this afternoon."

"I guess so," Cara answered, her brain rushing along. "We could take a walk or sit in the yard here. I could read to him. Would he like that?"

"Yes, he enjoys stories. That's wonderful. I'll drop him off at two o'clock." Mrs. Coobler paused. "I'm sorry to tell you, but the Teeners are bad-mouthing your club and putting ads in the newspaper about *mature* baby-sitters."

"I'm not surprised," Cara said sadly.

"I thought I should tell you that Paige sat with Pinky when he first arrived."

Cara repeated, "Paige sat with Pinky?"

Mrs. Coobler nodded. "I thought it'd be best to have an older sitter, but it didn't go well. I wouldn't have those girls ever take care of my children again!"

"I'm not surprised at that, either," Cara said. It was the second complaint she'd heard about the Teeners since she'd come home for lunch!

"I'd better hurry!" Mrs. Coobler said, "I'll drop off Pinky at two."

For lunch, Cara poured herself a glass of milk and, deciding against cheese and lunch meat, made a peanut butter and pickle sandwich. She sat down at the white-tiled counter and ate quickly. A good thing she was a "saver" and had saved her picture books.

In her room, she pulled out books Pinky might like. Angora glanced at her from the sunny window seat, then went back to sleep. Glancing at her alarm clock, Cara saw there was time to write in her journal. She pulled it out from between her mattresses, took a pencil from the cup on her desk, and flopped onto her bed.

Dear Journal,

Where is Jess's answering machine? I don't want to wait until we can talk to Garner McColl! I don't think he took it to get it fixed. I think Paige did this. But how? Arghhh!!!

I'm actually looking forward to baby-sitting Pinky Royster this afternoon. He's such a funny little guy. Only how am I going to ask him if he stole that money at Victoria Merrill's birthday party?

Just then, the phone rang and she hurried to the one in Mom and Dad's bedroom. "Hello, this is Cara—"

A woman said, "I'm calling about your ad in the paper for Teeners' Baby-sitting Service."

Cara drew an angry breath. "I'll have to take a message. One of the Teeners will call you back."

"Oh, aren't you one of them?"

"No," Cara answered.

The woman gushed on about "mature" baby-sitters. "The last twelve-year-old I had was asleep when we came home!"

Cara tensed. "I'm sorry to hear that—"

"Well, it was in another town," the woman admitted. "We've just moved here. Let me give you my name and number."

At least she isn't someone bad-mouthing the TCC! Cara thought. She got paper and a pencil from Mom's nightstand. If this wasn't the last straw, though! On top of everything else, she was taking job messages for the Teeners!

At two o'clock, Mrs. Coobler drove up with Pinky, and Cara stuck her journal between her mattresses, then ran to the front door, and outside.

"Pinky's so excited to spend the day with you," Mrs.

Coobler said through her car window. "I know you'll have a good time."

Pinky did look excited, his pale blue eyes sparkling.

"Come on," Cara said, opening his car door for him. "I thought this would be a good afternoon to read stories in our backyard, then maybe go for a walk."

Pinky beamed, and Mrs. Coobler said, "It sounds wonderful to me. Wish I could join you. See you!"

Cara had to laugh, then she led Pinky into the house. "Well, I see you're actually wearing shoes, and new overalls with stripes on them."

He grinned, then tugged off his leather sandals and began to somersault through the living room.

She didn't expect him to talk much, but he probably listened harder than most people did. "Come on, somersault kid. Let's sit out back on the patio."

Outside, he turned a few more somersaults, then actually settled on the white patio bench under the tree. She chose one of her old Grimm's Fairy Tales books and began to read *Rumpelstiltskin*. When she paused to look at Pinky, he was really interested.

"Sounds like the bad people against the good people, doesn't it?" she asked him.

He nodded.

Now was the time to ask him, she decided.

"I . . . I'd like to talk about something with you. Ummmmm . . . sometimes people who try to be good do bad things, Pinky."

Pinky listened carefully.

"After Victoria's birthday party, money was missing."

He looked down quickly, and she knew he was the culprit.

"Maybe you haven't been told that stealing is wrong, but it is," she explained. "Maybe sometimes when you were living on the street, you were so hungry that taking packs of raisins might seem right to you. But it isn't. Maybe sometimes you were so poor that taking money seemed right to you. But it isn't."

Pinky stared down at his small bare feet.

"I guess if you were homeless, you'd be scared about not having enough food or money, and that's how you'd get started taking it."

Pinky sat very still.

"It's not right, though," she repeated. "I don't know a lot about God or the Bible, but I do know that it says not to steal. If you took the money at Victoria's birthday party, I'd be glad to give it back to them from my money."

To her surprise, she added, "I really love you, Pinky."

He glanced up at her, tears in his eyes. Then he reached into the left side pocket of his overalls and took out a handkerchief with coins knotted in it. He offered it to her, handkerchief and all.

"Oh, Pinky!" She grabbed him in a hug. "I'm so glad you've admitted it. We're learning at church that truth always wins out." She wasn't so sure of it yet herself as far as Paige and the Teeners were concerned, but it seemed like a good thing to tell Pinky.

"We'd have time to take the money back now. You want to?"

He nodded hard.

"Come on! Let's get your sandals back on."

In the house, she took an envelope from the kitchen desk and put the coins from his handkerchief in it. "It'll be a long walk, but we can make it. Let's go."

As usual, Pinky was quiet, but as they walked along he pointed at birds twittering from the treetops and even flowers. She guessed that homeless people in the cities didn't see many birds, flowers, or even trees.

"We're lucky to be here, aren't we, Pinky?" she asked, and he nodded, smiling.

"Just look at the sunshine slanting through that tree."

He smiled even more widely, and she decided it was all right having a one-sided talk about nature.

When they arrived at the Merrills' house, no one was home. "Let's just push the envelope through the letter-drop in the door. What do you think about that?"

He'd been glancing around nervously, but he nodded.

"I'll just write on the envelope that someone took it and wants to return it. That's the truth, isn't it?"

"The truth," he said. "The truth."

"I'm proud of you, Pinky." She bent down and hugged him. "Really proud. I wish you were in my family instead of Paige!" He hugged her back hard.

When they returned home, Paige sat on the living room couch, waving her freshly polished fingernails. "Well, if it isn't a kid who can't even talk."

"Paige!" Cara warned.

"What do you mean, *P-a-i-g-e!*?" her half sister mocked. "That kid is a no-brainer. He's a loser. Look, he can't even understand a word we say!"

"He understands a lot!" Cara shot back. "I thought you were supposed to be baby-sitting now—"

Paige flounced off to her room and slammed the door.

"You'll have to forgive her," Cara told Pinky. "She's the brain-damaged one from being hateful. She's mean to me, too."

Pinky still looked hurt.

Cara glanced at the clock on the mantel. "Almost time for the TCC meeting! Could you make us peanut butter and jelly sandwiches in the kitchen for a snack? I'll get everything out, then I have to go to the bathroom."

She left him in the kitchen making sandwiches for both of them. When she returned, Paige was talking on the phone, her back to Pinky.

Paige was saying, "No way will *I* sit for that many little kids and change diapers, and I told Mrs. Stile that, too! Don't ever try to stick me with a job like that again. I'll see you at our meeting after dinner."

So Paige had walked out on her big sitting job, Cara thought. That definitely would be bad for their reputation.

Something else. Teener meetings were *after* dinner?! How could they baby-sit evenings if that's when they had their meetings? It didn't make sense.

"See you," Paige said, then hung up. When she turned, she asked Cara, "Well, what are you listening to?"

"I'm only in the kitchen with Pinky! By the way, there's a message on the board for you."

Paige grabbed it and stalked off toward her room.

When she'd slammed her door, Cara asked Pinky, "Did she say anything about an answering machine?"

Pinky shook his head, staying in quiet mode.

Moments later, Paige hurried to the front door, purse in hand. She called back to them, "The only good thing about the Twelve Candles Club is that you meet at Garner McColl's house!"

———

At four-thirty, Becky sat in the usual desk chair at Jess's house. "This meeting of the Twelve Candles Club shall now come to order." As if she suddenly realized something was missing, she turned to look behind her. "What's happened to the answering machine?"

"It's gone," Cara explained. "It was gone when I came here at noon. Dad says we may as well wait until Jess's brothers get home from work. Maybe they took it to be repaired. Or maybe it's still under warranty and the store will give them a new one."

"If someone stole it, you'd think Tumbles would have barked," Becky said. "Come to think of it, he's mighty quiet."

A dreadful thought hit. Cara slammed down her secretary's notebook and ran for the back window, Becky and Tricia at her heels. Cara pulled up the mini-blinds, and they looked into the white-walled doggy yard. "He's gone! Tumbles is gone!"

"He couldn't get out by himself!" Becky remarked. "He couldn't get under that gate!"

"We'd better call Garner," Becky said. "Jess wrote his work phone number on the chalkboard, just in case."

Cara headed for the phone. "I guess it's me, since Jess put me in charge of her room. Let's hope the phone works!"

She picked it up and was glad to hear a dial tone. Glancing at the green chalkboard, she punched in Garner's work number. Waiting, she told them, "I'll ask Garner if we should call the Animal Control Department, too."

In moments, Garner was on the phone and promised to be right home. "Yeah," he decided, "call Animal Control. Jordan and Mark had lunch with me, and I'm picking them up after work, so they couldn't have been home."

As soon as Garner hung up, Cara called Santa Rosita Animal Control. "I want to report a stolen dog," she told them.

"Stolen?" the man asked. "How do you know?"

"He's just a puppy, and he can't get out of a walled-in yard alone. No, he couldn't get under it or the gate, either."

The man asked endless questions, then finally took Tumbles's description. "I'll put him on the Missing Animals List," he said. "That's all I can do."

It didn't sound like much to Cara.

When she hung up, they all ran outside to look at Tumbles's doggy yard. There was no clue to show what had happened. They returned inside and phoned neighbors to see if any of them had seen him.

Nothing.

While they waited impatiently in Jess's room, Becky handed out the flyers she'd drawn the night they'd planned the club. "We have to get more around," she told them. "The way things are going, TCC has to start all over again."

"I made Mystery Week handouts, too," Tricia said. "We can give them out at tomorrow's neighborhood block party."

"Let's hope it gets us more Funners!" Becky remarked. "Jess and Melanie will be home Monday. Just two more days!"

Cara felt like crying. "Worst of all, we have a mystery right here about Tumbles. If we can't find him, it will break Jess's heart. What more could go wrong? What more?"

CHAPTER

9

The next morning, Cara rode her bike down the street to the Hutchinsons, the TCC's usual first car-washing job on Saturday mornings. But the next two Saturdays, the Hutchinsons would be away on vacation. Fewer jobs for TCC—again!

As she rode along, she recalled Garner McColl arriving in his green Bronco yesterday. He'd searched the house and the garage—and then the neighborhood with them. No Tumbles.

"Someone stole him," he said. "There's no other answer." He drew an unhappy breath. "Poor Jess. Tumbles was really her dog, more than anyone else's. Poor, poor Jess."

When they'd all given up, Paige ambled up the McColls' driveway. She wore her bright red sundress and matching lipstick. Her long bleached blond hair fell perfectly to her shoulders, meaning she had worked hard on it.

"What are you doing here?" Cara asked.

Paige gave her a hurt smile. "Why, I just happened to be out walking and decided to stop for you, little sister."

I'll bet! Cara thought. Paige looked too perfect to just happen to come along. Her eyes darted to Garner McColl. Not surprisingly, he looked at her, too.

Paige lowered her dark lashes at him, flirting. "Besides, I thought maybe you needed help."

"Help for what?" Garner inquired.

"Oh, just for anything. I saw you all wandering around as if you were looking for someone."

"For Tumbles, Jess's dog," Garner replied.

"I am very, very good at finding things," Paige murmured. "I could help you, Garner."

"I don't think so," he answered nervously. "Now, if you'll excuse me, I have to get back to work."

Cara had almost laughed, and Becky and Tricia hid their lips with their hands. Cara decided she would never ever flirt. It only made others laugh at you!

———

At dinner the night before, Paige had been very grouchy.

Now, riding her bike in the morning sunshine, Cara pulled into the Hutchinsons' driveway.

"Hey!" Tricia called from her bike. "You still asleep?"

"More like dreaming." She wasn't too surprised to see Pinky Royster hurrying along down the sidewalk, too. "Whoa, Pinky! I'm glad to see you. You want to help us wash cars?"

He nodded, grinning.

In the distance, Mrs. Coobler stood on the sidewalk and waved, probably making sure Pinky arrived safely. She'd phoned this morning, and Cara had refused to accept pay for Pinky hanging out with them. Besides, she and Tricia were it—the only ones to wash cars. Becky couldn't come.

Happily, Pinky grabbed an SOS pad to scrub cars' wheels—their least favorite job.

After the Hutchinsons' cars were bright and shiny, the three of them headed next door to wash the Matthews' white Honda. That left two more cars to wash as they worked their way along La Crescenta back toward Cara's house.

When they'd finally finished, she and Pinky returned home. Across the street, Paige's red Thunderbird was parked at the top of the McColls' driveway right next to Garner's green Bronco. Paige looked gorgeous in her black shorts and tank top, her blond hair drifting over her tanned shoulders.

"Hey, Cara!" Garner yelled down. "We have Tumbles back!"

She and Pinky ran up the McColls' driveway, and she was thrilled to see Garner letting Tumbles out of his Bronco.

"The Animal Control people found him," Garner told Cara. "Thanks to your thinking to phone them."

Tumbles wagged his brown tail so wildly that Garner laughed. "I guess Tumbles says thank you, too."

Paige stared daggers at her, but Cara stepped past her to pet Tumbles and to tell Garner, "This is Pinky Royster. He's staying with the Cooblers."

Garner offered his hand. "Hi, Pinky."

Surprised, Pinky shook Garner's hand.

Paige managed a cool "Hi" at Pinky, who eyed her warily. Tumbles wagged his tail at Cara and Pinky, then stopped as he looked at Paige.

Cara thought she must be mistaken. A puppy wouldn't understand unfriendliness, or would he? Even Garner seemed to have noticed, because his eyes went to Paige, then questioningly to Cara.

"If only Tumbles could talk," Cara remarked.

Paige lifted her blond hair high off her neck and batted her blue eyes at Garner. "Are you going to the block party this afternoon?" she asked, sounding hopeful.

"I hadn't planned to," he answered. "Will you be there?"

Paige beamed. "Oh, yes! In fact, I'm leaving in a minute so I'll be there early. I hope you'll come. I'd be glad to give you a ride."

Just then a loud "Rrrrrrivet!" croak came from Pinky's overalls pocket. Pinky grabbed for the frog, but it was already jumping onto the driveway. "Rrrrrrivet! Rrrrrrivet! Rrrrrivet!" He hopped under Garner's car.

"Ohhhh!" Paige squealed, heading for Garner's arms.

Tumbles barked and tore after Rivet. Garner dodged around Paige and grabbed Tumbles by the collar. "I'd better get Tumbles to his yard. He's probably never seen a frog before."

"Really!" Paige said. "I'll bet these kids set Tumbles loose, but they don't want to admit it."

"We did not!" Cara retorted. "Why would we do that?"

Pinky had rolled under the car, and now he rolled back out with Rivet. Glaring at Paige, he put the frog back into his pocket, then he and Cara marched away down the driveway together.

"Forgot to tell you," Garner called after them. "Jess's entire phone is now missing."

Cara turned back. "Her phone? You're kidding!"

Garner shook his head. "Believe me, I'm not."

"I can't believe it!" Cara exclaimed.

"We've decided to wait until our parents come home Monday to deal with it all," Garner said.

By then the club will be ruined, Cara thought. *Ruined!*

She was disappointed to see Garner head for Paige's car.

"It looks like this car will really go!" Garner remarked.

"It does," Paige laughed. "And I've got the speeding tickets to prove it."

Moments later, they drove away in Paige's car.

Cara trudged down the driveway with Pinky. On top of everything, they'd be late for the block party. At least they could eat lunch there since Mom was bringing take-out Chinese food for their family.

They headed south on the sidewalk to the farthest cul-de-sac, where La Crescenta ended and the yearly block party always took place. Before long, Becky and Tricia rode by on their bikes, wearing their grubbies, too. "We've got the handouts," Becky yelled. "Why aren't you riding your bike?"

"Pinky doesn't have one," Cara said. "We'll get there. You'd better write our phone numbers on the handouts. Jess's phone's been stolen!"

Becky almost stopped her bike. "I can't believe it!"

"It's true," Cara answered. "Garner wants to wait until

his parents come home to see what to do about all the trouble."

"I just have the strangest feeling that God's going to take care of all of this, one way or another!" Tricia said, riding on.

Becky said, "I'll stand on that, too." She rode on behind Tricia and called back, "See you at the block party!"

Cara didn't see any reason for being happy.

Finally she and Pinky arrived at the cul-de-sac. Over a hundred people sat in their folding chairs under trees or milled around talking. At the front curb stood the Teeners—Paige, Sandra, and Leigh—all dressed in fabulous black shorts and tank Tees. Their blond hair streamed over their shoulders, and they definitely looked like smooth, popular girls.

To everyone who passed, they said, "We'd like to introduce you to the Teeners Working Club. We give one free hour of baby-sitting for every five we do for you."

Why didn't we think of that? Cara wondered. Yesterday, with Tumbles missing, they hadn't even discussed lowering their prices for sitting or anything else.

The Teeners added, "We're mature teenagers, not twelve-year-old sitters. You can trust your children with us."

Cara almost spoke up, but Pinky squeezed her hand.

A new neighbor glanced at the Teener handout. "They're very nicely printed. Not amateurish like the others. Could you sit for our two girls tomorrow afternoon?"

Sandra Bassinger had a clipboard and wrote down the information right away. "Thank you. We'll phone after we've checked our calendars."

Paige told the woman, "We now give cheerleading lessons on Monday, Wednesday, and Friday mornings at our Teener Play-Care. All three of us are high school cheerleaders."

"Wonderful—my girls would love it!" the woman answered.

Uffffff! Cara thought. Little girls couldn't resist that. In the middle of the crowd, Tricia and Becky handed out both TCC handouts. "One handout is about our mystery play next week," they told people. "The other is about our regular jobs like baby-sitting, housecleaning, and car-washing."

Cara noticed Tricia's and Becky's Tees were as smudged as her own. Compared to the Teeners, the three of them definitely looked bad—like sloppy twelve-year-old car-washers, even though Becky hadn't been there.

———

Sunday morning, Cara rode to church in Tricia's family's mini-van. The good news was that Tricia's father attended church now too. The bad news was remembering their disaster at yesterday's block party: the Teeners had definitely outshone them.

"You okay, Cara?" Becky asked from beside her in the middle seat. "You look sort of white."

"Instead of Hispanic brown, you mean?" Cara flung back.

"No way!" Becky said. "I'm really concerned about you. You seem so worried lately."

"Sorry," Cara answered. "I'm just upset about the Teeners, and Paige being part of them."

"Tricia still says all things come together for good to

those who love the Lord . . . that we need to turn more to Him when we go through trials," Becky explained. "I know I sure do. I've turned the whole club over to Him. And you know what—I even feel good about it. I can't explain it, but something good will come of this. I just know it."

"Maybe that's what I'm doing wrong," Cara said. "I'm not turning to God. But I keep worrying about Jess and Melanie coming from Israel tomorrow and finding out the club is ruined."

"Pray about it," Becky said. "Really pray about it."

The rest of the way there, Cara tried to forget about the Teeners, and tried to turn the Twelve Candles Club over to God. But *trying* didn't lift her spirits.

In the church parking lot, Cara, Tricia, and Becky headed for the youth room. Once in it, Cara was glad to see the youth pastor, Bear, was alone, writing on the greenboard.

"Hey-hey, Cara!" he began, cheerful as ever. He was short, broad shouldered, and in his flowery shirt and baggy pants, he looked like a cozy Teddy Bear.

"I have an important question," she said and rushed on. "Does . . . does truth always win out when someone has done you wrong? And when that someone is a liar?"

He turned serious. "If not here on earth, then later. Our spirits are accountable to God. The Bible tells us that liars have no place in Heaven."

"You mean when we die?"

He nodded. "Yes, when our spirit goes on to be with Him."

"It'll be too late by then," she said, mostly to herself.

"Trust Him," Bear said.

"Thanks anyhow," Cara answered, then trudged away to the sit with Becky and Tricia.

Before long, Bear played his guitar for their singing. Praise songs did make her feel better, Cara decided, reminding her that someone else—someone a lot more powerful—was in charge. If only she could trust Him with all of her heart like Tricia and Becky seemed to. If only . . . if only . . . if only. . . .

Monday morning another "only" hit. Only five Funners attended Morning Fun for Kids. Craig Leonard said, "The girls are off with the Teeners for cheerleading."

"That's all right," Tricia answered. "We're going to have a mystery play, and even Pinky and his frog, Rivet, are going to be in it. What do you think of that?"

Becky clapped and cheered, and Cara joined in with the Funners, but her heart wasn't in it. The only good part was Pinky's somersaulting.

"What's the mystery play about?" Craig asked.

"I don't know yet," Tricia admitted. "I'm still praying about that. Does anyone have ideas?"

It wasn't like Tricia to be unprepared for something so important, Cara thought. It seemed as if the club were sinking deeper and deeper into trouble.

Tricia said, "Jess and Melanie will be home in a few hours. Maybe they'll have the mystery play idea for us."

Cara didn't feel hopeful.

Dear Journal,

It's Monday afternoon, and Morning Fun for Kids didn't go well. But my real question is: How did someone get into Jess's room to steal the answering machine? It must be the same person who let Tumbles loose and then stole the phone.

I don't see how Paige and her friends could get into Jess's room with the door always locked. How would they get a key? Somehow the Teeners got the names of almost all of our clients and know about our jobs, too. Sure, my newspaper article told a lot, and Paige heard me talk about jobs. It's so depressing.

Jess and Melanie are coming home in one hour. We've canceled the TCC meeting to go meet them at the church. How can we ever tell them the bad news?

———

The silvery tour bus carrying the Israel group home drove into the Santa Rosita Community Church parking lot, and the crowd waiting for them cheered.

Becky's gram had brought her and Amanda to pick up their mother and new step-father. Auntie Ying-Ying and Uncle Gwo-Jenn came for Melanie and her parents. Tricia's mother brought Tricia and Cara to welcome their friends home, and Pinky was with them. The McColl boys came for Jess and their parents—and Paige was probably there to see Garner McColl.

The bus chuffed to a stop and the front door flapped open.

"Yeaaaahhhh!" everyone shouted. "Yeaaaahhhhh!"

Cara clutched Pinky's hand. "No somersaulting."

The bus driver got off the bus first, but Jess was right

behind him, looking as short, tan, and athletic as ever. "Whoa! Look at everyone!"

Melanie climbed down behind her, surprised to see so many people, too. But she was more restrained as suited a beautiful Asian-American model. "I can't believe you'd all come!"

"Guess what?" Jess asked. "We were both baptized in the Jordan River! And so were Mr. and Mrs. Llewellyn! And you can't believe what people ate over there!"

"The trip was wonderful, just wonderful!" Melanie added. They moved aside for the other passengers to get off, then everyone was hugging friends and family members. Becky received extra big hugs from her mom and new step-father.

As they waited for the bus driver to unload bags from the storage compartment under the bus, Jess said, "We wished you could all have been there. Did you get our post-cards?"

"No, not yet," Becky answered. "Gram says it takes longer for postcards from Israel. They'll probably come next week."

"What's new?" Melanie asked Cara. "What's happening with the Twelve Candles Club?"

Cara's heart sunk. "Nothing good."

"What do you mean, *nothing good*?!" Jess asked loudly.

People all around them seemed to listen.

Tricia explained, "There's a new club called the Teen-ers, and they're trying to get our business."

"Everything's gone wrong," Becky added. She told Jess, "First, your answering machine was wrecked, then it was stolen. And now even your phone is gone!"

Cara said, "And Tumbles disappeared, but we got him back!"

"You're kidding!" Jess exclaimed.

Cara shook her head. "The worst part is that Paige is in the Teeners, and they've stolen most of our clients. We hardly have any jobs left. Except for cleaning Mrs. Llewellyn's house next Thursday, we have no cleaning jobs all week." Cara's heart hurt, and she blinked back tears.

Nearby, people were listening, and Mr. and Mrs. Llewellyn had just gotten off the bus. "Why, hello, girls!" Mrs. L said. "How lovely to see you! Wait 'til you hear all about our trip!" She paused and stared through her thick glasses. "What's all the fuss about?"

"Another club called the Teeners has stolen our jobs," Cara answered. "They just stole them."

Indignant, Mrs. Llewellyn said, "You girls will have jobs with me forever . . . or at least until my cleaning woman's well."

Cara glanced back through the crowd and saw Paige smirking. She stood with Garner McColl, holding his arm as if she owned him. Worse, he was looking pleased about it. He wasn't even going forward to greet his family.

As everyone else stood visiting with their families, Auntie Ying-Ying called out, "I have announcement . . . very big announcement." She waited in her red silk Chinese dress, waving her hands for quiet.

"I got big surprise! Big job for Twelve Candles Club! My friend, she own travel agency. In one week, she want Twelve Candles Club girls for cruise ship job. In one week . . . all week on Caribbean cruise they baby-sit ten passengers' childrens. I go, too. Want to wait 'til Melanie home to tell you."

"The week after next!" Cara exclaimed. "I'll have to ask my dad. We wouldn't have to cancel much—"

Tricia whooped, then turned to Mrs. Llewellyn. "What about us cleaning your house?"

Mrs. Llewellyn gave a laugh. "Forget it! Go on that cruise! Believe me, that's what I'd do!"

Cara, Jess, Becky, Tricia, and Melanie stared at one another. "A Caribbean cruise!" they shouted, not quite believing it. "A Caribbean cruise!!!!"

Paige had pushed through the crowd and stood glaring at them. "It's not fair! The Teeners are older! We should be going on the cruise, not you stupid twelve-year-olds!"

"You stole our clients!" Cara flung back. "I'll bet *you and your friends* messed up Jess's phone and answering machine, then even stole them and let Tumbles loose! I'll bet you even got that phony letter-to-the-editor in the paper to knock us!"

A new thought struck. "You took my key and had a copy made! A copy! That's how you got into Jess's room!"

"So what if we did!" Paige yelled. She was so mad, she didn't even know what she'd said. Garner McColl edged away from her, though, and hurried away to greet Jess and their parents.

In the silence that followed, Pinky yelled, *You're a bad sitter, Paige! You said on your phone that you hate kids!*

Paige eyed Pinky with amazement, then looked around and saw everyone seemed to believe him. "Well!" she huffed, then whirled away and stalked to her car.

Cara felt a great surge of relief. The mystery had been solved. It was over.

Melanie asked, "What's that all about?"

"We have lots to tell you," Cara answered, "and, believe me, we won't have to cancel many jobs to go on the cruise."

Tricia gave her a high five. "And we'll have our jobs back when we get home. After this, everyone in town will be wise to the Teeners."

Almost without thinking, Cara exclaimed, "Truth really does win out! And this time, on *earth*. Yeah!"

Her friends cheered, too, making Pinky somersault around them.

————

Later that night, after Cara and Becky and Tricia had had a long visit with Jess and Melanie, Cara settled down in her bedroom and wrote in her journal.

I actually feel sorry for Paige. She tries so hard to get good things happening in her life, but her bad attitude and dishonest ways always spoil things for her. Not only can she make other people miserable (like me!), but she must be miserable, too. I finally see that. Poor Paige, she doesn't know that God loves her. It seems weird, but Becky and Tricia were right about the TCC all along, and they had peace because they could feel the love of God. And because of their faith, I know better that He loves me, too!

Filled up with love, Cara said aloud: "I forgive Paige." It was the second time this summer she'd forgiven her half sister, but it felt good to have done it.

Probably there'd be plenty of chances to forgive Paige again. What was it Bear had read from the Bible about how many times to forgive? Seven times seventy! Four hundred and ninety times to forgive Paige! Yipes, what if the rest came all in *one* day? Now that would really be a miracle, just like truth winning out today.